"We can't do this..."

Damian's eyes glittered. "I want you."

It was a bold-faced statement that rocked Mia and, dear heaven, aroused her.

She closed her eyes briefly. "It would complicate things. This was supposed to have ended days ago."

"Nothing says it couldn't be more." He quirked his lips. "You want me...but you don't trust me, is that it?"

Sweet heaven, he was blunt. "Has anyone told you that subtlety is an art form?"

"You're the artist. I'm just a businessman."

"Please." He wasn't *just* another entrepreneur.

He bent to kiss her again, and she pushed against his chest.

The Musils and Serenghettis were going head-to-head in business again. If only her brother knew that she was standing in Damian Musil's arms right now and fighting the urge to get naked with him.

Sometimes family loyalty could be a kick in the pants...

* * *

So Right...with Mr. Wrong by Anna DePalo
is part of The Serenghetti Brothers series.

Dear Reader,

Welcome to the Serenghetti Brothers—four powerful, passionate Italian American siblings. Mia Serenghetti is younger than her brothers—Cole, Rick and Jordan— but though she's last, she's certainly not least!

Up-and-coming clothing designer Mia moved to New York City and away from her loving and protective family in Welsdale, Massachusetts, in order to launch her career and, more importantly, forge her own identity. It's too bad that she lands in the arms of Damian Musil, the scion of the Serenghettis' longtime rivals in the construction business. Damian is a budding media mogul, so he knows synergy is everything. He offers to be Mia's escort to a gala because it would be good business for both of them. Then one evening ends in bed, and this dealmaker who plays for keeps gets so much more than he bargained for. When the conflict between the Serenghettis and the Musils heats up, can Mia trust that Damian isn't just opening up the latest front in the battle between the Musils and the Serenghettis?

Warmest wishes,

Anna

PS: You can find me on my website at annadepalo.com, on Facebook at Facebook.com/AnnaDePaloBooks, on Twitter at Twitter.com/Anna_DePalo and on Instagram at Instagram.com/AnnaDePaloAuthor.

ANNA DEPALO

SO RIGHT...WITH MR. WRONG

HARLEQUIN

Desire

Recycling programs
for this product may
not exist in your area.

ISBN-13: 978-1-335-23287-8

So Right...with Mr. Wrong

Harlequin Enterprises ULC
22 Adelaide St. West, 40th Floor
Toronto, Ontario M5H 4E3, Canada
www.Harlequin.com

Printed in U.S.A.

Books by Anna DePalo

Harlequin Desire

The Billionaire in Penthouse B
His Black Sheep Bride
One Night with Prince Charming
Improperly Wed

The Serenghetti Brothers

Second Chance with the CEO
Hollywood Baby Affair
Power Play
So Right...with Mr. Wrong

For Antonella, Alessandra & Valentina

cugine di sangue e del cuore

One

When she finally spotted the guy she'd been look-ing for, Mia knew there was only one thing to do—especially when she had less than two weeks to find a date before the Ruby Ball, an all-important fash-ion industry event, and her would-be escort had just married someone else.

She stepped from the alcove where she'd been lurking. The rooms on the top floor of the Brooklyn brownstone were dimly lit and otherwise deserted—all the other costumed partygoers were downstairs or in other rooms, mingling and laughing with the Halloween-obsessed hostess whose birthday it was. It was a cool spring evening, but the air on this up-permost level felt warm.

The man turned toward her and pocketed the cell phone he was holding.

Though a dark mask covered the upper half of his face, the height and build were right.

Sam. He'd given her only few hints about what he would be wearing.

"Look for me in a plain costume," he'd said with a quick grin. "I'm not one for lots of glitter."

She'd spotted him in the throng downstairs and had made her way across the crowded parlor floor when she'd seen him ascend the stairs. By the time she'd caught up with him on the sparsely furnished top floor, he'd had his back to her and had been speaking in a low voice into his cell phone—business call, no doubt. So she'd lurked beyond an open archway in an empty adjacent room, pretending as if she hadn't been stalking him. Waiting for him to come into sight again once he finished his call.

Mia pulled up the shoulder of her dress, which had a bad habit of slipping off. Unlike Sam's, her costume was anything but understated. The black-and-red concoction was all ruffles, with the skirt cut high in front—showing off her fishnet-clad legs—before dipping low in the back.

She and Sam had flirted at a couple of parties, and he'd brushed her lips with his when they'd last seen each other. It was all the encouragement that she'd required. She needed a new boyfriend *fast*—or at least someone who could pass as one.

The Ruby Ball wasn't only an *it* fashion event, it was also one where everyone came as a couple—the better to burnish their images and brands. Unfortunately, in a fit of bravado at the most recent Fashion Design Newcomers meeting, she'd let it be known that she *was* showing up with an escort—even if it wasn't her erstwhile boyfriend, since Carl was now very much married.

She had to pull this off. She *would* pull this off. As long as she had the guts. Time to accelerate her acquaintance with Sam…

He looked up in surprise as she stepped toward him. His dark eyes were shadowed in the low light cast by a table lamp.

With a sudden shot of nerve and adrenaline, she used gentle pressure to bring his head down and pressed her lips to his in greeting, taking up where they'd left off.

He stilled. But after a moment's pause, his hands settled on her waist, and he brought her more fully against him. His mouth moved over hers, caressing her lips and then settling deeper. His tongue touched hers, played with her.

She linked her arms around his neck, giving herself up to the encounter. This guy knew how to kiss—he put everything into it—and as she started to pull away, he followed, stroking her parted lips, coaxing a further response.

She made an involuntary sound in her throat and let him deepen the kiss.

His scent was deliciously warm and clean, and in counterpoint to the hard and lean body that now pressed against her, fitting to her curves and enveloping her.

Her heart thumped in time to the rhythm of the music reverberating through the house.

OMG. This was not what she'd been expecting. The last time they'd brushed lips, she'd gotten no clue about the smoldering heat that Sam could bring out in her. Maybe her plan wasn't so crazy after all...

When they finally broke apart, she sighed. *Wow*.

"Hi, Sam," she whispered.

"Who's Sam?"

She froze.

The voice was definitely *not* Sam.

Her eyes widened, his narrowed.

Then he lifted his mask, and Mia sucked in a breath.

Damian Musil.

She slammed the door on her inner wail and pushed away from him as if she'd been burned.

Why? Why did it have to be him of all people?

After years of sidestepping the enemy, she'd fallen into his arms—or thrown herself there. She winced inwardly.

There was no hint of surprise in his expression. "Do you always kiss masked men in dark rooms?"

"Don't be absurd," she snapped, covering her mortification. "Obviously it's a case of mistaken identity, and you know it."

"Who's Sam?" Damian asked again, his shadowed eyes betraying nothing.

"None of your business."

"I disagree, since minutes ago we were locking lips."

She took a deep breath, which served only to push her breasts up and draw his attention—*damn him*.

"Oh, right," she said sarcastically, "I forget that you like to warn away the guys I date."

"That's one way of looking at it," Damian responded.

Her temper sparked. Carl's small and quick wedding had had few guests, but since Damian had once been Carl's boss, he had been one of them. He'd supported her boyfriend's decision to break up with her for a kindergarten teacher he'd had a kismet moment with on a plane ride.

Sure, she and Carl hadn't been serious. After meeting at a party, they'd dated for three or four months. But his dumping her and immediately marrying someone else had still stung. Especially when she'd discovered through friends that Damian had encouraged the whole thing.

She wanted to stamp her foot and rail at the fates, which had left her not only boyfriend-less on the eve of one of her life's key moments, but now had her locking lips with the man responsible for her plight. How much humiliation could one woman take? And how could she ever have thought of Damian as attractive, even in passing, back in her teenage days?

He was several inches taller than her own five-foot-seven and built like a lightweight boxer. With a square jaw, dark hair and brown eyes blazing intelligence, she figured some women would say he packed a double or triple threat.

But she knew that he could be calculating and ruthless. Just like what she'd always been advised to expect from a Musil…

She raised her chin. "One way of looking at it? I suppose the other is that you were opening another front in the war between the Serenghettis and the Musils?"

He had the temerity to look amused. "Is that what you think?"

The Musils were her family's business nemesis, ever since her father, Serg Serenghetti, had suspected Damian's family of underhanded tactics to make it in the construction business and undercut competitors in western Massachusetts—namely, Serenghetti Construction. The bad blood had gone on for years.

Because Welsdale wasn't a big place, she knew Damian's real name was Demyan but that he went with the English instead of Ukrainian version. And once upon a time she'd even looked up its meaning: *tamer.* But she vowed that he wouldn't be taming anyone, especially a Serenghetti. Her family loyalties ran deep—even if she was known as the wild child.

In the years since high school, she'd moved to New York City to work in fashion and start her own label. And Damian had become a billionaire app developer with his startup company. She wondered darkly whether he'd succeeded in his chosen field only with the dodgy business tactics for which his family was known.

Musil. She remembered Damian correcting everyone back in high school. *It doesn't rhyme with mussel, it's Musil like Mew-seal.* Nowadays, there was no need to correct anyone's pronunciation. Everyone knew his name.

Mia straightened. It was time to end this meeting, instead of standing close together in the dark—as if this was some kind of clandestine romantic encounter.

"I need to go. I'm on my way to—"

"Look for an escort to the Ruby Ball. Right."

Mia's eyes widened. *He knew?* Things had suddenly gone from bad to worse.

Damian shrugged. "I overheard Nadia and Teresa talking earlier."

Mia muttered something under her breath.

"What are friends for, right?" He could still pick up her scent, feel the imprint of her curves, taste her on his lips...

"I'm not going to discuss this with you." She swung away. "In fact, this conversation is over."

"Which one?" he drawled. "The one about you kissing me? Or the fact that you're here to find someone other than Carl to accompany you to a career-making social event?"

She gave him the side-eye—looking for all intents like a woman who'd discovered a bug in her morning coffee.

"And they say the Musils are calculating."

She narrowed her eyes. "You are."

"Don't forget *dastardly* and *underhanded*."

"Those weren't the words I was thinking of," she remarked with a saccharine smile, "but thanks for supplying some nicer substitutes."

He cut off a laugh.

She swept him with a cool look. "Great costume. The masked villain is so appropriate."

"It's a Robin Hood costume." The character had been an easy and fast online pick.

"And considering that you're the reason why I need a substitute date," she went on, ignoring him, "I expect you to laugh diabolically at your victory."

He lifted the side of his mouth to get a rise out of her. "Or offer a lending hand because you're low on options. I'll check my calendar but a week from Saturday should be clear."

Mia parted her lips in a huff. "Not if you're—"

"—the last man on Earth. I know."

She threw up her hands. "Obviously you can't take a hint."

"Your signals have been more than a hint." He remembered her mouth under his. Soft, hot, sweet. She'd put real feeling into it—before she'd known who he was. And from what he'd been able to observe when they'd been around mutual friends and acquaintances over the years—first in Welsdale and now in New York City—Mia dove into everything with heart and soul.

Holy hell, after years of crossing paths with aloof

and wary steps through a shared hometown and overlapping New York social circles, he'd finally settled any speculation about what it would be like to kiss Mia Serenghetti…and he hadn't let the opportunity pass him by. He hadn't even had time to think about why she'd suddenly come on to him. His jaw ticked at the thought of the unknown Sam, and he damned the other man to eternal oblivion.

Because right now Mia was a fantasy come to life dressed in a costume that a Las Vegas show girl might have worn. The outfit set off her shapely legs, long rich mahogany locks and almond-shaped moss-green eyes thickly fringed beneath sculpted brows.

His body tightened. The floor reverberated with music and laughter from below, but up here they were alone… If they were dating, he'd buy her the most outrageous sinful stockings. Lacy, black and sexy. And then he'd taste her full, cherry-painted mouth again while she wrapped her legs around him…

Wisely, though, he kept mum about all of it. "Listen, I had nothing to do with Carl marrying another woman."

"What?" She sucked in an outraged breath, which lifted her breasts. "I suppose supporting his breakup with me so he could hook up with someone else constitutes *nothing* in your book."

"It was what Carl wanted to do."

"But you gave him the encouragement he needed. You held the match to the powder keg."

Damian rubbed his chin. "That's a colorful analogy."

She raised her eyebrows. "It's accurate. You even offered him a private plane so he could get to Martha's Vineyard for his honeymoon."

He'd wondered what Mia had heard about his interactions with Carl—and what her reaction was. Now he knew. "You've got an outsized view of my influence."

"I'd say a plane qualifies as big," she snapped.

"Carl is happy."

"Because of you."

"Maybe," he admitted.

"And we'll never know whether he'd have gone for it without your help."

"I told him to follow his gut."

"Yes, and apparently that meant breaking up with me. Did it give you perverse satisfaction that a Serenghetti was going to take a hit in the process?"

"I've got nothing to do with JM Construction these days. That's my father and brother's gig."

She snorted. True, the family-owned construction company must be small fry to him these days, but she wasn't fooled for a minute. "Right, you're the tech founder with major bank...so I wonder why you'd care what a Serenghetti is doing or isn't."

"You're insisting this is about some ridiculous Serenghetti-Musil family feud."

"Isn't it?"

In his opinion, Mia and Carl hadn't been a good match. Mia was a take-charge type. A dynamo. Carl was a laid-back guy who strummed his guitar and was happy as a supporting player in one tech company after another. Hell, Damian had even employed the guy for a while and then had recommended him for an opportunity at another company.

But Carl had been in existential angst about switching girlfriends. So when the guy had asked his opinion over a couple of beers, Damian had given it.

"You're upset because the breakup with Carl happened right before a big event," he said calmly.

"No, I'm upset because your meddling caused the breakup with Carl to happen right before a big event."

"A situation I've offered to rectify for you."

She clenched her hands and then released them. "So you're the good guy? Un-believ-able."

He pointed to his costume. "Call it my hero complex."

Mia blew a breath, causing tendrils of hair to lift and resettle.

"If you're Robin Hood, what does that make me? Maid Marion?" she asked frostily.

Knowing it would provoke her, he scanned her ruffled costume, which revealed both leg and cleavage. "You don't look the part."

"Exactly."

"Too much fiery temper."

She frowned, annoyance stamping her face, before she smoothed her brow. "I agree, and that's why your offer would never work. I've got outfits in mind for the Ruby Ball, and, let me tell you, nothing about them says they're right out of Sherwood Forest."

"Let me guess. Instead you're the femme fatale and your escort is—"

"Not you."

Under Damian's bemused gaze, she whirled away and stomped off.

But whether Mia liked it or not, their kiss couldn't so easily be left behind...

Two

He was the most infuriating man she'd ever met, and that was saying something considering she had three older brothers.

Mia pushed hair out of her face and looked around her cramped design studio, where her cousin Gia—who'd dropped by because she'd come to the city for a business meeting—was perched on a stool and responding to a text.

She'd tried to make a frank point to Damian about his help to Carl and their sparring families, and instead *he'd* reduced *her* to noting that Robin Hood didn't apply to their situation…

She caught herself touching her fingers to her lips *again*—the memory of their kiss was hard to erase—and yanked her hand back down. This whole situation was making her crazy…and desperate.

Gia tucked her phone away and regarded her levelly, picking up their conversation where they'd left off. "Are you out of your mind?"

Mia acknowledged there was no good answer, and that her chaotic surroundings hardly vouched for her sanity. Bolts of fabric were propped against the wall, a sewing machine was jammed into one corner, along with an ironing board, and there was hardly a place to sit. The buttons that she'd recently bought sat in a box nearby, and she knew she'd have to make another trip to Mood Fabrics. On the other hand, she was lucky. Many newbie designers worked right out of their apartments. At least she'd been able to rent a studio a couple of floors below her own one-bedroom walk-up in the Garment District.

"I know that asking Sam to reschedule his business trip to Singapore is a Hail Mary pass—"

"The Serenghettis play hockey, not football," Gia interjected, her hazel gaze doubtful.

Mia hadn't even confided in Nadia and Teresa at the party after her encounter with Damian. Now her fashion school friends were half a world away, having flown out for a cruise of the Mediterranean before they headed back to jobs at different clothing labels in Milan. And she was here, finally rehashing the experience with her cousin…

"I haven't misplaced my brain, if that's what you're thinking," Mia continued. "And for the record, it's my brothers who play hockey, not me. Jordan might still be in the NHL, but Cole stopped. And Rick never played. He was a wrestler in high school."

"Still, no football in the genes," her cousin said, shifting on her seat. "Face it, you haven't got the aim to complete a pass with low odds of success."

As if on cue, Mia's phone vibrated, and she snatched it off the table. She processed Sam's text, and her shoulders slumped. "Well, it was worth a shot."

With an *I told you so* expression, Gia folded her arms.

Mia sighed. Sam had eventually shown up at the brownstone party on Saturday, but before she could bring up the Ruby Ball, he'd announced that he'd be out of the country for two weeks. "Sam can't reschedule his business trip. Apparently, the timing is right for him to meet up with some of his former fraternity brothers in Japan."

"And you can't afford a guy who is into a boys' trip like *The Hangover*," Gia pointed out. "You already have a hangover."

"I don't have a hangover. I have a headache." One that was about to get much worse unless she came up with a date soon.

Her cousin nodded. "Yup. A sign you're a workaholic. You should be having fun to go along with the whole female empowerment message of your brand."

"Why do you think I need a date?" She tapped her finger against her mouth—glad that this time it wasn't because of the memory of a certain kiss lingering on her lips. "Maybe I can hire an escort..."

"Dear sweet heaven, girl, no. Why don't you find a male model to attend with? Isn't that an old PR ploy designed to get publicity?"

"First off, the Ruby Ball is a fashion industry event. Someone would probably recognize him from some photo shoot or other. Also, I don't merely require an escort. Preferably, I need an image boost with someone...impressive."

Sam had qualified, sort of, because he came from a well-connected family that had made its fortune in banking three generations back, even if Sam himself was a midlevel music exec.

Rats. She'd started her fashion label, MS Designs, for the modern woman ready to slay today—but thanks to Carl, she was looking like the furthest thing from her own target demographic.

"Isn't there a hockey player or somebody that one of your brothers can recruit?"

Mia rolled her eyes. "The last thing I'd do is ask one of my brothers to help me find a date." It would be a humbling experience, even apart from the teasing, especially given her long quest to stake her independence from her family. "Anyway, Jordan's team isn't in town on the night of the Ball, so it would definitely be an imposition."

"Well then, give Damian a chance," Gia said. "He fits the bill, and you said he's volunteered. Ask him. It's not like your family pays attention to the fashion press anyway."

Mia suddenly regretted sharing details of her run-in with Damian at the costume party, but she and Gia were as close as sisters. They were almost the same age and in artistic fields—Gia was a cartoonist with a widely circulating strip. And of course, they had rhyming names—which had led to no end of jokes over the years, particularly from Mia's brothers. "Maybe you should start the Damian Musil fan club."

Gia shrugged. "Alex likes him."

Gia's new husband was a millionaire in the tech field, so of course he'd crossed paths with Damian.

"Alex doesn't have the history with the Musils that the Serenghettis have," her cousin added, pushing back her newly straightened dark hair.

"Exactly. Anyway, I don't know how seriously to take Damian's offer to be my date. He might have just been needling me." Entirely possible given the Serenghetti-Musil feud. "And do you know how my family would react if they ever discovered I showed up as a couple with Damian?"

"When have you ever let that stop you?" Gia countered. "Isn't *rebel* your middle name?"

Right. The Serenghettis of Welsdale, Massachusetts were all about construction—and hockey. And more lately, Hollywood, thanks to her middle brother, Rick, and his movie star wife, Chiara Feran. So naturally, Mia had gone to New York to study and work in fashion design…because her rebellious streak had started early and extended beyond triple-pierced ears.

Mia sighed again. She could have tried to attend with a friend, but she'd done a quick inventory, and she didn't have any guy friends that were completely unattached at the moment. But Damian...?

"You'll be seen by lots of people at the Ruby Ball, though." Gia worried her lower lip.

"I'd dump him the next day," Mia said jokingly. *ASAP.*

Then she paused, her eyes widening in reflection.

"What are you thinking?" Gia asked suspiciously.

The idea of going out with Damian and then making it seem as if she'd dumped him quickly, if necessary, was gaining traction. Maybe a plan of attending the Ruby Ball with him wasn't so risky after all...

Mia bit her lip. "You know," she said thoughtfully, "the idea has some appeal."

Gia's eyes widened as understanding dawned.

"If anyone asks, our relationship had a quick and unfortunate end."

"Who's going to ask?"

"Oh, you know, if the question ever comes up." With any luck it wouldn't. But a few of the platitudes that celebrities relied on flashed across her mind like a Times Square news ticker. *We uncoupled, but I wish him nothing but the best. I've grown and learned so much from past relationships about what I really want and need in a partner.* The last was about subtly shifting the narrative, of course, without outright placing blame on the party who'd fallen short. She really needed to stop reading gossip sites…but then again, wasn't her brand about encouraging women to seize their power?

"Okay, how are you going to handle your family if they find out?" Gia rolled her eyes. "They'll be shocked."

Try horrified. "And relieved the dating was over in the blink of an eye. They'd be more worried if Damian was still in the picture."

Gia shook her head. "Okay, well, I'm glad you've realized Damian is maybe your best option for the Ruby Ball. As to everything else, there are ways this plan can go wrong."

"Now you're having cold feet?"

"Think of me as your living, breathing conscience making you think things through."

"Yeah—like when I suggested sneaking backstage at that concert," Mia muttered, the memory still fresh in her mind twenty years later.

"Hey, I told you it was a bad idea."

"Security was already chasing us in the arena's restricted access tunnel when you said that."

"Well, it was worth a shot at meeting the Backstreet Boys," Gia replied.

Yup. And her brother Jordan had done much more hell-raising back then—and she'd had a thing to prove about there being nothing her older siblings could do that she couldn't. "I guess you have a point there. Nothing ventured, nothing gained."

Still, Damian Musil?

* * *

There were upsides to being your own boss. Today was not one of them.

Damian rubbed the back of his neck and then leaned back in his office chair.

Absently, he nodded to one of his managers who walked past beyond the glass wall of his office and saluted him with his takeaway coffee cup.

Victor broke his stride and poked his head in the door. "See you at the meeting at 11."

"I'll be there," Damian responded, noting the time at the bottom of his computer screen before the manager disappeared from view.

Frankly, Damian figured a meeting would be a welcome distraction right now.

He needed to hire a new exec to head his video streaming service, FanvaTV, and his messenger app—the core of CyberSilver, the company that he'd built—was running into software difficulties. He'd just read an email detailing the bugs that still needed to be worked out in the planned software update.

And *that* was only his work life. He wondered again if Mia had ever caught up with the mysterious Sam on Saturday night, and his jaw tightened.

He swiveled to face the window behind him, staring pensively over Madison Square Park below.

The trees were getting foliage, and the stray puffy white cloud was no match for the sun at midday. The occasional cherry tree added a dot of contrast to the deepening green canopy below. Everything was ripe for new beginnings—just like he'd felt once.

Ten years ago, when he'd taken his small inheritance from his mother and moved to New York City to start his business, he'd envisioned being here someday. Except things were supposed to be easier when he was flush with success. He'd spent years building, running, forgetting. To get as far away from his parents' hardscrabble existence as he could. And yet…

He still had problems, including his biggest one at the moment. With his growing new media company, CyberSilver, some might wonder why he was interested in an aging local television company. But to him, buying the privately owned station in western Massachusetts would be the ultimate validation of his success. Yes, he'd left the family construction business to his father and brother, but buying back into the Massachusetts market in a big way would mean the Musil name would become associated with more than JM Construction.

The potential television station acquisition was personal on his part. A first…since he never let emotions influence his corporate decisions. But the satisfaction from owning WBEN-TV, along with the couple of other New England stations that came with it, wasn't something to be dismissed lightly… If only he could get the owner to sell to him.

Larry Bensen was suspicious of someone who had no background in television broadcasting, even if Damian owned a new media company and had roots in Massachusetts. Larry was ready to retire, but only if he could leave his company in good hands—since no one else in his family was interested in running it.

The truth, though, was the guy needed to sell to a bigger player. Larry had done everything in the past few years to keep his company competitive, including bringing in new management. But big conglomerates ruled media, old and new, these days. And Damian's biggest worry was that Larry would sell to someone else.

Especially since Larry's requirements included vetting a potential buyer's character—because he wanted a buyer who'd treat his company as if it were a family inheritance. Considering that Damian came from a fractured family and wasn't even close to starting one of his own—he wasn't even dating—that requirement put him at a distinct disadvantage. He was too tied to his job to have much of a social life, so at least he didn't have much in the way of negative publicity—no reality stars, baby mamas or lingerie models willing to tell all for the right price. But, on the other hand, he wasn't a poster boy for domesticity, either.

Damian idly reached for the computer mouse and reopened the email from Larry that he'd gotten that morning.

I'll be in NYC next week for the Ruby Ball. Katie is covering it for *Brilliance* magazine, and Allison wants to go. Let's meet if you're in town.

Damian shook his head. Yup, Larry was all about family. He'd even named Alley Kat Media, his holding company, for his wife and daughter, Allison and Katie. And now Larry was coming to town because his daughter worked for a fashion magazine and his wife, a former model, was interested.

Damian turned again to stare thoughtfully out the window, and his lips quirked. This was the second time in a week that the Ruby Ball had cropped up as a topic of conversation in his life. Days ago he'd teased Mia about accompanying her to the celebrated event…

She'd turned him down, of course. Because she'd been bred to distrust and look down on a Musil.

But his body had hummed ever since their last encounter, when finally, finally, he'd been able to taste her lips. And the kiss had been hotter and better than he'd ever expected. She was a beautiful woman—growing into the potential that had been evident back when she still lived in Welsdale.

And lately, every time their paths had crossed, Damian had found her to be even more compelling and fascinating.

Damian steepled his fingers. He suddenly had a business interest in attending the Ruby Ball. He had not been able to get Mia off his mind, especially since Saturday's kiss, but now Larry would also be in town for the event…

No matter what Mia thought, however, the Musils weren't underhanded so much as ruthless. The business sense he'd learned from his family had served him well. He had more power and money than he'd ever dreamed of.

Damian contemplated his office view. Maybe it was time to cast doubt on everything that Mia heard about Musils over the years—as well as having her owe him one. In some ways, he couldn't have planned things better if he'd tried.

It looked as if he and Mia might be headed toward another rendezvous… He had only to beat the mysterious Sam to it…damn it.

Damian searched his mind for where he'd last crossed paths with Mia before the costume party. He knew a local trendy nightspot that was the usual haunt for some of their mutual acquaintances. He'd try there first on Friday night.

And with that thought, he straightened in his chair and leaned forward to reply to Larry's email.

Three

She was nursing dashed dreams but congratulating herself on her principles…so the last thing she needed was for temptation to walk through the door. But then, Mia had never felt especially lucky.

She watched with trepidation as Damian strode into the Twilight Club, as if he felt comfortable and welcome anywhere.

She'd temporarily separated herself from some acquaintances and gone to the bar for a drink. She'd seen Damian here in the past, but not so frequently that she'd been worried about him showing tonight…

Ask him. Gia's opinion sounded in her head.

Ugh. One week left till the Ruby Ball and of course enticement would walk in to test her resolve. She'd continued to waffle and had all but decided that Gia's suggestion of asking Damian was just too crazy—despite some of her brave words to her cousin—but now here he was...

Before Mia had a chance to make any decision, however, Damian strode right to her and parked himself at the bar, as if he too had been mulling a mission.

He nodded at the now-empty glass of Coke at her elbow. "Buy you a drink?" Then not waiting for an answer, he signaled the bartender. "Beer on tap. The darkest you have. And another round of soda for her."

"You like to take charge." She made the observation grudgingly.

"I'm a CEO."

"So am I." She, however, did not have the same pull. Already a couple of women had recognized him and were throwing sidelong looks in his direction.

Damian smiled at her. "How's it going with Sam? Have you run him to ground yet?"

Must he be so annoying? "Hardly. He's on a plane to Singapore."

"And the airline's departure gate closed before you got there?"

"Wouldn't you love it if I said I barely avoided arrest trying to stop him from boarding?"

He flashed a grin. "Somehow I doubt that's the kind of publicity you're looking for."

The waiter put her soda down on the counter, and

she took a sip. "No publicity is bad publicity. Isn't that what they say?"

"I like a woman who goes after what she wants. So what's your backup plan?"

She eyed him. "What makes you think I have one?"

"Well, since I'm standing in front of you," he drawled, "I figured you'd be considering contingency options."

Damn him. "You?"

He nodded, leaving his beer untouched. "Me. As it happens, I now have a business reason to attend the Ruby Ball, and something tells me you have an extra ticket."

"I'll sell it to you."

Mia's mind buzzed with the pros and cons of Gia's idea all over again. She'd tried to convince herself that Damian had been merely joking at the costume party—but now he clearly wasn't. On the one hand, she was desperate, as much as it irked her that he knew it. And actually, did she have any other choice? On the other hand, Damian was a Musil. Her family would have a joint conniption if they found out. Even if Damian wasn't in charge of the family construction business, he had been and probably still was a beneficiary.

Then again, she'd never let family disapproval stop her, as Gia had pointed out. In fact, she'd often run into its open arms.

Like right now. Oh, Damian didn't literally have

his arms open, but the man was…seductive. He seemed to know her weak spots.

She wavered. He waited.

Desperation won out, even if she was still suspicious. "Why would you be interested in an event that's all about high fashion?"

He quirked his lips, his expression rueful. "I'm not, but my client is. His wife was a model before they married. Now they're ready to retire, if they find the right buyer for their business. I aim to be Mr. Right."

Mia rolled her eyes. "So you're going to trot out your date, the fashion designer." *Me*.

He looked amused. "A bonus I wasn't looking for."

She figured it was a testament to her recent history with men that being referred to as an unexpected bonus didn't faze her. And Damian was a Musil, after all—she should keep her expectations low.

"And as it happens, a bonus for you, too. My client's daughter is covering the Ball because she's employed by *Brilliance* magazine."

Mia drew in a breath. He obviously knew she'd jump at the chance to make a connection at one of the foremost fashion magazines around. *Damn it*. Temptation had taken an irresistible turn.

Sure, she had some connections of her own—namely through her sister-in-law, actress Chiara Feran—but the whole point was being independent of her family. She wanted to make it on her own, not trade on her name, though she had done some cross-promotion with Chiara's former stylist, Emery, who'd started her own accessories line. And while her sister-in-law had friends in Hollywood who were walking billboards for designers, what Mia needed at this point wasn't simply to lend out her clothes for free publicity, but to expand her retail reach with department stores and boutiques. And for that she needed industry connections…fashion editors, store buyers, word-of-mouth in the trade. Anything that would get those orders coming in. Yes, she'd hired a publicist but her budget was no-frills, and fashion was a competitive business—she needed to work every angle.

Before she could let herself dwell on it any more, she blurted, "If anyone asks after the fact, I dumped you."

Paradoxically, mild amusement stamped Damian features, and then he quirked a brow. "Should we shake hands on it?"

He was playing her, using his bargaining skills. But she knew some of her own. "The can-can girl and the villain?"

He laughed, not missing her allusion to their recent encounter at the costume party. "Sounds like the name of—"

"—a low-budget movie." A disaster flick, hers. With the subtitle *Mia Runs Out of Options*.

The minute her palm came into contact with his, however, awareness shivered up her arm and spread outward.

Her lips parted, and she took a quick indrawn breath.

Damian held her gaze and the world fell away.

Why did she always have such a sensitized reaction to him? And what would it feel like to come into closer contact? Feel his lips on hers again and have him caress her with his hands while she moaned her pleasure... *OMG, no.*

It was bad enough that she was attracted to him even if she didn't totally trust him. Determinedly, she slipped her hand from his, and he let her go.

For now.

But there'd be a next time—the thought came unbidden.

Mia sipped her cocktail and regarded her youngest brother carefully.

Jordan was in town. *Rats.*

Sometimes one of her brothers visited New York. Usually not her oldest sibling, Cole, who now ran Serenghetti Construction. Occasionally it was her middle brother, Rick, who was a big-shot Hollywood movie producer—and still had plenty of contacts in New York City from his days as a Wall Street money man. Most often it was Jordan—her youngest brother and the older sibling closest to her age— since he played professionally with the New England Razors and traveled for his NHL away games.

Usually she was thrilled to see him, but the timing right now was awkward at best.

Since the Razors normally stayed at the Renaissance Hotel, which was a stone's throw away from her place in the Garment District, she didn't have a good excuse not to meet. And because the late afternoon was nice and sunny, they were meeting in one of the hotel's popular locations—the Versa restaurant, with its impressive indoor/outdoor seating, retractable roof, potted greenery, and glass walls overlooking Midtown. She was glad at least that they weren't at the Renaissance's Thread Bar, since its fashion theme attracted a like-minded clientele— namely, people she was likely to know. Right now, there was only so much she could handle without someone in the industry mentioning the Ruby Ball in front of her brother. As it was, she'd had to swear Gia to secrecy...

"I thought Cole was coming to town this week. He mentioned he had one of those once-in-a-blue-moon business conferences."

Jordan's lips quirked. "He'd planned to, but the Musils are up to no good again."

Mia's stomach turned over, but she managed weakly, "Oh, really? I haven't heard a thing about the Musils in a long time."

Liar. Liar. But did Damian count if he wasn't in Welsdale anymore?

Jordan nodded. "They've been quiet, but now they're bidding to buy the same construction company, and for Cole it's personal."

Mia knew that Cole was looking to expand Serenghetti Construction in order to stay competitive. Construction was increasingly a business where the big players had an edge—and the little guys faced the threat of being left behind.

"Oh, please," she said lightly, "Cole's grow-or-die philosophy hardly means it's personal."

"For Cole, it's more than that. JM Construction has been a thorn in his side ever since they almost got the construction deal for that new gym."

Mia knew JM Construction was named for Damian's father, Jakob Musil. She'd learned that fun fact the way other kids learned their alphabet...because she was a Serenghetti. She shifted in her seat. "Oh, come on, Cole should be thanking the Musils. If JM Construction hadn't had the upper hand, Cole would never have volunteered to headline the fundraiser that Marisa was organizing for a new athletic facility at the school where she works. He would never have mended his relationship with Marisa, and they'd never have gotten married. There was a silver lining to the competition with the Musils."

Jordan's lips quirked. "In other words, the Musils did Cole a favor? I don't think he sees it that way."

Damn it. Why did the business rivalry with the Musils have to flare up right now? "Doesn't Cole have enough going on without worrying about the Musils? After all, with your plan to fund a new wing at the Children's Hospital, Serenghetti Construction will have more than enough business."

"Again, Cole doesn't see it that way. Besides, with existing projects, Serenghetti Construction is already stretched to the limit. If he wins the takeover battle, it'll ease some of the strain on resources."

Oops.

"Anyway, let's talk about you," Jordan said, seemingly oblivious.

Let's not.

"How are you doing?" He took a sip of his beer.

Mia waved her hand. "Oh, you know, business as usual."

Her brother quirked a brow. "You're leading the glamorous fashion designer life in the big city, and you don't have anything happening? Yeah, I believe that."

She had to get them off this topic fast. "You'll be surprised like everyone else when I make a splash."

Her brother laughed. "Okay, fair enough." Then he sobered. "It's nice to see you in a better mood, Mia. After Carl, we were all worried about you."

"Well, don't. Worry, that is. Carl is in the past." *And I've got bigger things to worry about these days.*

Jordan shook his head. "If I ever run into Carl—"

"You'll say hi and keep going. I can take care of myself." She'd escaped to New York, but sometimes it didn't seem far enough from her protective relatives. Sure Jordan was showing he cared, but she'd also been assigned a place in the family tree, and no one seemed interested in having her change her position.

"Maybe be choosier about who you date."

"Right." *Starting after Saturday.* "Says the guy who used to be a major player before he met his wife."

"Exactly. I speak from experience."

As a big NHL star, Jordan had gotten his share of headlines, including at least one woman trying to shake him down for his money and celebrity.

"I'm not a big enough designer to attract hangers-on."

"You will be."

"Thanks for the vote of confidence."

"In the meantime, better luck spotting the duds."

She shrugged. "It's New York City. There are literally thousands more single women than men in this town."

Jordan smiled. "Don't I know it. Or at least, I used to."

Mia wagged a finger at him in jest before they both sipped their drinks. The youngest of her brothers used to be in the running for hockey's most eligible bachelor. Tall, with dark hair and green eyes, he'd made women breathless with his underwear billboard ads.

Seriously, Jordan was in no position to judge... even if she did show up in public on the arm of a Musil.

And Damian might be many things, but he wasn't a dud. The guy had major bank, industry respect and name recognition.

On top of it, she'd been working weeks toward the Ruby Ball. And plans were finally falling into place, sort of...

Four

She'd gone bold for tonight, and her outfit was just the start of it. The pink top was shaped like a suit jacket except the deep V in the front revealed what looked like the top of a red bustier but was actually the cleverly accented bodice of her dress. Below her waist, a pink satin skirt was open at the front in a deep inverted V that revealed long, shapely legs encased in red satin to match the bustier. The whole ensemble set off her dark mahogany hair and tanned complexion.

If she wanted to invite attention, best to go all out, right? She'd designed and made the gown herself, even though MS Designs focused on ready-to-wear—at least till now—and not haute couture. No use advertising someone else's design chops instead of her own if she was dreaming big. And if news filtered back to her family about the Ruby Ball, maybe her daring gown would divert some attention from her date. *Maybe.*

Still, Mia's bravado nearly deserted her when Damian closed the limo door behind her and she stepped forward on the pavement.

One intense look from him and her pulse kicked up. Her heart beat faster, and shivers of awareness danced over her skin.

Automatically, she touched the ruby resting above her cleavage, and his eyes became hooded. He'd invited her to make a loan appointment at a discreet Upper East Side shop and pick out matching jewels. He'd had access that she could only dream of, but despite some misgivings, she hadn't been able to resist.

Now that both she and Damian were dressed to thrill, however, she wasn't prepared for his effect on her senses. And the short limo ride from her apartment, where he'd picked her up, had done nothing to dull it—*drat.*

He looked hot, dark and intense in an impeccably tailored tux over a black satin shirt and tie. It was a modern, edgy look that complemented her dress. But though she'd given him some sartorial pointers when they'd communicated by text in the days leading up to the Ruby Ball, she wasn't prepared for the finished package. *What had she been thinking?*

He was big and tall, and he practically smoldered. It was one thing when they crossed paths at a party or bar, it was another to handle Damian at a public event that she couldn't walk away from.

He led her forward with his hand at the small of her back—the imprint radiating out like warm, undulating waves carrying her off to…

Focus. Mia straightened and smiled as they approached the building entrance. The Vanderman Mansion was a New York landmark that often served as an event space and backdrop to some of the city's most lavish parties.

"Relax," Damian murmured. "You look stunning."

She cast him a side look. "Amazing how you can say that while smiling. Where did you learn ventriloquism?"

His smile broadened. "In the boardroom. You never know when you'll run into a lip reader when you're negotiating a business deal."

She let him guide her forward. "So that's the Musil trade secret?"

"There are others."

After running the gauntlet of reception, they stepped inside the event space, where sequined gowns and crystal chandeliers competed for dazzling allure.

Damian took two champagne flutes from a passing waiter and handed one to her.

"Cheers," he said, clinking his glass to hers. "You made it."

Mia took a deep breath and then a sip of her drink.

"Original design, by the way," Damian said, making the compliment sound both casual and incendiary.

How did he do it? Mia resisted the urge to blow a breath to cool her face. "I made it myself. MS Designs."

"Of course," he murmured. "Red suits you."

She cast him a sidelong look from under her lashes but was spared a reply as an older couple approached.

The gray-haired man clapped Damian on the shoulder. "Damian, good to see you. Not your crowd, I think, but glad you were able to make it."

"Of course," Damian replied smoothly. "How could I miss an opportunity to attend the Ruby Ball?"

Mia flushed because only she could know Damian's tongue-in-cheek meaning.

Damian turned toward her and made introductions to Larry Bensen and his wife, Allison. "Mia is a designer with her own label. MS Designs."

Allison leaned toward her, her chestnut hair gleaming. "It must be so exciting to have your own brand. I did some modeling when I was younger, but I was always fascinated by design. I never got beyond some fun sketches."

Mia smiled. "I hope you held on to those designs. What goes around comes around in fashion."

Allison laughed. "These days, our daughter Katie is the artistic one. She's why we're here tonight. She's covering this event for *Brilliance* magazine."

Larry cast an indulgent look at his wife. "No,

we're here because you never lost your love of fashion. And I told you that your bolero jacket was the right choice for tonight."

Allison smiled at her husband, and then tugged at the lapel of the jade satin jacket that she wore over a beaded gown. "After more than thirty years of marriage, you've become an expert."

Larry chuckled. "Yes, but I also read *Brilliance* magazine because there are copies all over the house."

Damian looked around. "Speaking of which, where is Katie?"

"Working," Allison answered. "Or I should say, working the room and interviewing guests about their outfits for tonight."

Damian kept his smile in place and nodded toward Mia. "Then she should interview Mia."

Mia flushed again. "Now that's—"

"An excellent idea." Allison craned her neck as if looking for her daughter. "I'll try to wave Katie over."

"Allison likes her role as Katie's personal assistant," Larry joked before glancing from Mia to Damian. "So I guess you have a connection to the fashion world, too, Damian."

To Mia's surprise, Damian's arm circled her waist, and he pulled her closer. "Mia fills me in."

Larry looked thoughtful. "I like that you're getting out of the office." He cast a loving look at his wife. "Allison cured me of my workaholic tendencies a long time ago, and my doctor gives her credit for helping me avoid another heart attack."

"We stay active," Allison chimed in. "We play golf with another couple on weekends at a club between Welsdale to Springfield. Do you play Mia?"

"Er—yes." She wouldn't call her golf game anything but passable, though she'd learned to swing a club thanks to her brief stint on the high school golf team.

"You and Damian should join us one weekend," Larry put in. "Nothing like a little friendly competition, right?"

Mia blinked with a fixed smile. A golf date? She and Damian were ending their fake relationship after tonight.

"Mia comes from an athletic family," Damian said teasingly. "I wouldn't discount her skill on the golf course."

Just then a petite young woman came breezing up.

"Katie, there's someone I'd like to introduce you to," Allison began. "Damian is a business associate of your father's, and Mia is a fashion designer."

Katie gave her a sweeping look but her expression was friendly as they exchanged greetings.

"Are you based in New York, Mia?"

Mia cleared her throat. "Yes, and I have my own label. MS Designs."

She forced herself to stop and not blab. *You probably haven't heard of it.*

Katie tilted her head. "Mmm, I think I've heard of it."

Mia flushed. "I've done a few shows."

"More than a few," Damian put in.

Mia looked at him quizzically—was he trying to bolster her, or had he really been keeping tabs on her career? She found the latter hard to believe…

Katie tilted her head. "Great dress. Original, and the cut and tailoring are super. One of your own designs?"

"Yes, but right now, I market casual wear."

"Why don't you get in touch?" Katie said. "I know Editorial at *Brilliance* is always looking to shine a light on promising new names."

Mia smiled. "Fantastic."

She felt herself relax as Katie turned to her parents to chitchat.

Damian put his hand on the small of her back and leaned close. "Nice job. Your first contact of the evening."

For one wild moment, Mia thought he was referring to his touch at her back, but then she collected herself.

"Maybe my only contact," she responded lightly.

"Never underestimate."

Mia tingled, but there was no more time for private conversation.

Katie blended into the crowd again with a quick goodbye, and Larry addressed another question to Damian.

Mia glimpsed at Damian's smooth profile, which contrasted with the tux's darker hue.

His advice could just as easily apply to him. Because it wouldn't be wise for her to underestimate Damian Musil...

Hell, he should have anticipated Larry might complicate things. So here he was the next day, waiting for Mia to show up at the midtown café where she'd agreed to meet him at his request.

Damian shifted in his seat and then took a distracted swallow of his coffee.

When he'd gotten back to his place last night, his mind had buzzed with thoughts—fantasies—of Mia. Her dress had suited her—all red and pink and fiery just like her. And what had looked like a push-up bra peeking from beneath a satin jacket had played havoc with his concentration. He'd itched to unbutton her, spread those lapels, and let his mouth and hands roam those gorgeous breasts.

A snatch of conversation between them from the end of the evening replayed itself in his mind.

Are you sure you don't need help getting out of that dress?

I'm a fashion designer. I know all the tricks.

Too bad there's nothing I can teach you.

Just then, as if called forth by his thoughts, he looked up to see Mia walk in.

Today she was flushed and a little windswept, her lips rosy. The body-hugging jacket accentuated her curves, which were encased in leggings and knee-high boots. It was cooler and windier this afternoon than yesterday, and she'd obviously dressed accordingly.

As she sat down across from him at the small café table, he slid a cup toward her. "I ordered for you while I was waiting. It's lemon-scented chamomile tea, but if you prefer something else, I'll put in another request."

Her eyes widened fractionally.

"I noticed last night that's what you asked the waiter for at the end of the evening."

"Observant."

He wondered what she'd say if she knew he noticed everything about her. At the costume party, even in the dim light, he'd gotten close enough—finally—to notice that her eyes had a subtle mismatched green hue, and that her scent had been light but sexy and sultry. He'd never paid attention to a woman's scent before, or had it linger to haunt his thoughts.

Mia took a small sip of her tea, her eyelashes lowering, and then she sighed.

Damian shifted in his seat.

Setting her cup down, she looked up.

Their gazes clung for a moment, and she must have read something in his because her lips parted on an indrawn breath. Finally, she broke eye contact, and leaned down for the small brown shopping bag that she'd parked next to her when she'd sat. "Before I forget again—" she said, passing the bag to him "—thank you for arranging for the jewelry. I would have brought everything back today myself but the jeweler is closed on Sundays."

He was slightly amused by her haste to reassure him and cut ties. The ruby-and-diamond necklace, along with chandelier earrings, had suited her—emphasizing the vibrancy of her look. He couldn't have picked out something better himself. Mia had impeccable taste and a discerning eye.

Taking the bag and depositing it next to him, he said, "No worries."

She sat back with a glad-that's-taken-care-of look.

"But the jewelry isn't why I asked you to meet me."

Her eyes widened fractionally.

"How are we going to handle the invitation from the Bensons?" he asked, shifting gears to what he considered the real topic at hand.

She expelled a breath and brushed aside waves of dark brown hair that had fallen over her shoulder when she'd reached down. "Simple. One of us is going to fake illness."

"You've been thinking ahead," he remarked dryly.

"One of us has to."

"You know, it would be to both our benefits to go through with the golf date."

She blinked. "Near Springfield? That's like the backyard for the Serenghetti-Musil family feud. Springfield is mere miles from Welsdale. Are we trying to widen the conflict?"

"That's up to you, but I'm thinking that Larry

and Allison will want us to be on the same team. So they can, you know, beat us soundly."

"I'm not a regular golf player."

"You've got athletics in your genes. And anyway, we want to give them a run for the money but not embarrass them." He quirked his lips. "Bad for business."

"And here I was showing up today to publicly dump you," she replied tartly.

Somehow Damian wasn't surprised by her announcement. Still... "Why? Are you motivated by revenge or just distrust?"

Her eyes flared slightly. "You're blunt and direct."

"Comes with the business acumen." He curved his lips. "It's also where the instinct to look for additional mileage from our situation comes from."

"We agreed to attend the Ruby Ball together. That's all." She shrugged. "Before we get our families' hackles up."

"Ah."

"What? You don't care?"

He settled back in his chair and they bumped knees under the table. "I left Welsdale years ago. And so did you, come to think of it."

She leaned forward, a slight frown marring a face that could turn heads. "The Serenghettis and Musils are currently bidding to buy the same construction company, in case you didn't know."

He kept his expression neutral, even though it was bad timing for things to get stirred up between their families. "I don't know anything about it. I told you I'm not involved with JM Construction."

"But your family is."

"And you seem to worry a lot about what yours will think for someone who's struck out on her own in New York."

She seemed momentarily taken aback by his insight, but recovered quickly, her lips compressing.

Damian pressed his advantage. True, they'd agreed on showing up together only for the Ruby Ball, nothing more, but Larry had thrown a wrench in things. "We both stand to gain by accepting the Bensens' invitation. You get to curry favor with the parents of an important fashion editor, and I get to keep a potential business partner happy."

"I've already met Katie Bensen," she protested. "Last night. You're the one with more on the line here."

"A good businessperson isn't swayed by emotion…and that's what going our separate ways right now would be, especially when there's more to be gained by doing the opposite."

Mia jutted out her chin. "What about the satisfaction from tossing you aside?"

Over Mia's shoulder, Damian saw Carl walk in and cursed under his breath.

Mia followed his gaze, and her eyes widened. Then she swung back toward him. "Did you plan this?"

He quirked a brow. "No. The gods are laughing at me right now."

What the hell was Carl doing here? This was a trendy café, and both he and Carl—like Mia—lived in Midtown, but he must have run into Carl here only once before.

Before Damian could figure out what to do, Carl spotted them. Surprise, confusion and then shock flitted across the other man's face. After a momentary hitch in his pace, though, he started toward them.

Damian sighed. Carl had spotted them—of course, he had—and as awkward as it might be, there was no way to avoid the upcoming exchange of empty pleasantries.

Damian stood, smiling, and Mia got out of her seat, too. "Carl."

"Damian. Mia." Carl's tone was all fake jocularity. "This is a surprise."

"I was thinking the same thing." Damian slipped his arm around Mia's waist and felt her stiffen fractionally—but she didn't pull away.

Carl's gaze traveled between the two of them, and he shook his head bemusedly. "I got married, and you and Mia end up together. Go figure. Guess everyone winds up happy, huh? I mean now that I'm no longer standing in the way of everything getting sorted out."

Damian cursed underneath his breath as Mia gave a tight smile. *Carl needed to stop talking.*

As Mia opened her mouth, Damian cut in. "Mia and I were grabbing some tea."

It was the truth—though not all of it. As a non sequitur, it would work though.

Carl looked momentarily puzzled. "Well, I guess I'll be going. Just stopped in for some coffee. Two light roasts." His gaze passed from Damian to Mia and back. "Nice to see you."

When Carl moved away, Damian followed Mia's lead and sat back down. Neither of them said anything for a few minutes. Mia sipped her herbal tea, and Damian glanced out the window at the passing crowds.

It was only after Carl had gotten his order and departed that Mia raised her eyebrows and fixed him with a look. "Really?"

Damian didn't even pretend not to understand. "If your relationship had been serious, Carl might have had a different reaction right now."

"Or maybe he finally met the right person," Mia responded, something indecipherable flitting across her face.

"That, too," he acknowledged with a tip of the head. "Either way, it would never have worked. Carl's too easygoing for you."

"Meaning I'm not good-natured?" Mia demanded.

No, you're hot, hot, hot. Just like his scalding cup of tea had been...until she'd walked in and everything else had faded in comparison.

Damian quirked his lips. "You were upset about the timing of the breakup, but the Ruby Ball went off without a hitch for you."

"Yes, except now there are other problems," she muttered. "Larry and Allison think we're a couple, and now Carl does, too."

"Don't tell me it doesn't give you some satisfaction to have him think you've moved on," he murmured, keeping his voice down as other patrons took a seat nearby.

Mia leaned forward. "Of course he thinks so. You put your arm around me."

"And you didn't move away."

A look of exasperation crossed her face.

"You're fiery. Carl is relaxed. And a little clueless."

She arched a brow. "Unlike you?"

"I'm willing to learn."

"On a golf course?"

He smiled. "If necessary."

She rolled her eyes. "You've got it all figured out, haven't you?"

Five

Mia ran the comb through her hair using the entry mirror in Damian's Welsdale condo while he took a business call in another room. It had been windy on the golf course earlier.

She felt as if she were still a teen in high school—and it wasn't a good feeling. The problem was that she was sneaking around, trying to make sure none of her family knew she was almost on their doorstep right now—with Damian Musil. Except for Gia, of course—but then, her cousin had always been her partner in crime.

And so far so good. No one in her immediate family had called or texted. The Ruby Ball was a longstanding event, but important only in fashion circles. She was counting on it being a distant memory if and when her family found out that she'd been there with Damian Musil. By then, of course, she could maintain that she and Damian had long since parted ways—for good.

Early this morning, she and Damian had driven up to Massachusetts in his Lexus SUV. Fortunately it had been a beautiful sunny day—the weather had been perfect if a bit nippy—and the golf game had gone well. She and Damian had held their own even if they'd ultimately lost.

Afterward, they'd ended up here at the condo with the Bensons for drinks. At first she'd been taken aback—preferring to socialize at the course's clubhouse—but then Damian had clearly wanted to show off his local ties to Larry.

She'd also wondered idly if today's loss at golf had been an unusual event for Damian. He'd been so successful in his career, he probably hadn't experienced a true setback in years. Then she'd realized that he likely still thought of the day as a win. After all, before he'd left minutes ago, Larry Bensen had shaken hands on an agreement to a deal.

She deposited her comb in her handbag, which she'd placed on the console table below the mirror. As soon as Damian was done with his phone call, she was getting out of here—texting her mother that she was on her way over in a ride service, allegedly from the bus terminal.

As far as her relatives were concerned, she was coming up by bus sometime today for a short visit. She'd felt too guilty about not seeing them while she was in town, even if it made more sense to sneak back down to New York with no one the wiser. She'd fudged a little bit about when and how and why—the *other* why—she was coming up to town.

Still, as soon as she and Damian had driven into Welsdale after golf more than two hours ago, the back of her neck had pricked with the uncomfortable awareness that she might run into someone she knew...and would have to do some quick explaining—or covering up.

And right now, she didn't need any more curveballs. Her early morning drive up to Massachusetts with Damian had been eventful enough—and another silver lining to dropping in on her parents was that she'd avoid a similar ride back to New York. She'd been acutely aware of being confined in a small space with him, unable to ignore his strong and capable hands flexing on the steering wheel... the clean, masculine scent that she'd come to identify as his...and worst of all, his big frame folded into the seat next to hers. And then thoughts of their kiss had intruded again...

"Do we need to put on a show of affection for the Bensens?" she'd blurted.

He'd glanced at her from the corner of his eyes. "Just be yourself—"

She'd relaxed her shoulders.

"—unless, of course, you'd like to touch me."

She'd looked at him sharply and realized he was teasing.

She stared at herself in the mirror again. *Ugh.*

This was getting so complicated, and Damian was getting under her skin. The condo seemed too small to avoid temptation.

Time to leave.

She wondered when Damian would be done talking to whomever he was talking to. She supposed she could sneak out of here—but that would be rude, wouldn't it? And really, did she want Damian to think she was skulking away? No, she was a Serenghetti. Resolute and resilient.

She glanced around the luxury condo. She remembered when this complex had gone up in Welsdale while she'd been in high school. Of course, Damian would pick one of the ritziest addresses in town. The decor was understated, but her designer's eye had picked up on the telling details of luxury—the slate floor in the kitchen, the white marble in the bath… Naturally, though, Damian, had chosen a building that hadn't been built by the Serenghettis—or JM Construction, come to think of it.

"Great job on the golf course," Damian announced, startling her.

She turned to watch him approach while still tucking his phone away. He loomed large and impossibly magnetic.

"You did most of the work." She could be magnanimous—and she'd bet he wasn't expecting that from a Serenghetti. At the same time, though, she fished out her own cell phone from her handbag. Time to text her mother that she'd be at her parents' door soon—they'd agreed she'd show up before dinnertime—and then summon a ride.

"I guess I'll have to give you lessons."

She didn't let herself think about what else he could teach her…and accidentally dropped her cell phone.

Flustered by her clumsiness, she bent to retrieve it.

Damian mirrored her move, and they bumped into each other.

After making a grab for the phone, she straightened and mumbled, "Sorry."

Could things get any more awkward?

"Are you all right?" His voice was low, soothing, concerned.

He gently rubbed her temple where they'd hit, and her breath caught.

She looked up and searched his gaze. "Yes."

"Mia."

Suddenly, it was as if all the pent-up sexual tension of the day—the car ride, making nice in front of the Bensens, breathing the same air alone in a quiet condo—snapped free of its taut hold.

Awareness sizzled between them. Desire and unmistakable need stamped his features, and Mia feared her own expression mirrored his.

His gaze dropped to her mouth.

"Are we about to bump lips, too?" she blurted.

He smiled slightly. "We can claim it was another accident."

As his head lowered, she said, "Or a victory celebration…except we didn't win the golf game."

"We gave them a run for the money, that's what counts," he murmured. "It would have been bad form to beat a potential business partner."

"If you say so."

"Mia, can we stop talking?"

And then he gently angled her head and covered her mouth.

She sighed against his mouth, and then snaked her hands around his shoulders, anchoring them both.

His lips moved over hers, searching, seeking, testing. The kiss quickly turned hotter, needier and more desperate.

Pressing against him, she felt the unmistakable sign of his arousal. Her breasts crushed against his chest, fueling their need.

He backed her against the foyer wall, and she rested her arms on his shoulders, tangling her free hand in his hair.

If this kept up, they'd soon end up naked right here inside his front door. The thought flashed through her mind, bringing her back to sanity, and she broke the kiss.

Gulping in a breath, she forced herself to say the obvious. "We can't do this."

A muscle ticked in his jaw, and his eyes glittered. "I want you."

It was a bald-faced statement that rocked her, and dear heaven, aroused her.

She closed her eyes briefly. "It would complicate things. This was supposed to have ended days ago."

"Nothing says it couldn't be more." He quirked his lips. "You want me...but you don't trust me, is that it?"

Wow, he was blunt. "Has anyone told you that subtlety isn't your strong suit?"

"You're the artist. I'm just a businessman."

"Please." He was *just* another entrepreneur in the same way that New York Fashion Week was just another garment industry event.

He bent to kiss her again, and she pushed against his chest.

She remembered Jordan's words—the Musils and Serenghettis were going head-to-head in business again. If only her brother knew that she was in Damian Musil's arms right now and fighting the urge to lose control with him. Right here. Right now.

Her cell phone vibrated, and she pushed away.

She punched at her screen while Damian continued to stand there, the personification of sex...

When she read her message, however, she groaned.

You're dating Damian Musil. What the hell.

Cole's text was like a dousing with icy water. She seemed to be on a bad luck streak these days, and the timing of her brother's message couldn't be worse. She was in Damian's apartment, in Welsdale, and her family had no idea she was in town.

Guilt ate at her.

Damian clasped her upper arms. "Mia—"

"I have to go." Then she added, "The cat's out of the bag with my family."

"Wha—"

"Cole thinks we're dating. Apparently my brothers have suddenly started reading *Women's Wear Daily* or some other fashion industry press." A brittle laugh almost bubbled up.

She swung toward the door, not bothering to deposit her phone back in her handbag, and with her other hand, grabbed the overnight bag that she'd brought in with her earlier. Anything to give the impression of the happy couple for the Bensens' sake, right? *Liar, liar.*

Mia winced inwardly. If she'd been able to forget for a moment who she was and who Damian was—while she'd been losing herself in his arms—reality had come crashing back.

And it looked as if she was overdue for an interesting family reunion…

When Mia arrived at her parents' Mediterranean-style home outside Welsdale, she immediately recognized her brother Cole's pickup on the circular driveway that wrapped around a central fountain. It was joined by Jordan's expensive SUV.

The sky overhead had darkened with rain clouds, as if foretelling the turn that today would take from her sunny outing this morning with the Bensens.

Damn it. She'd been hoping she could speak to her parents first before tackling Cole. But she should have realized that her brothers might be here. It was a weekend, after all, and both Cole and Jordan were local.

Cole lived close by—in a house he'd built for Marisa and their preschool-age daughter, Dahlia. He'd only taken over Serenghetti Construction after their father's stroke a few years ago.

These days, her father instead appeared on local television with *Wine Breaks with Serg!*—short slots devoted to wine recommendations and connected to his wife's cooking show. Mia was proud her mother had started a second career with *Flavors of Italy with Camilla Serenghetti*. Everyone, it seemed, was finding their niche except for her. But she was trying.

After depositing her overnight bag by the front door, she braced herself and entered the spacious living room. Cole turned to face her, while Jordan continued to lounge with deceptive calm in an armchair.

Her brothers shared the same dark hair and tall build, but Jordan's eyes were green while Cole's were hazel. And Cole had always been bigger, bulkier and rougher around the edges—his nose having been broken once.

At least her parents weren't in sight—yet.

"Are you nuts?" Cole asked, standing in the middle of the room.

"And hello to you, too, Cole," Mia replied dryly. "Thanks for not wasting time with pleasantries."

"Why bother when you've lost your mind? Showing up at a public event arm in arm with Damian Musil?"

"At least you've saved me the effort of filling you in." Mia eyed her brother but kept her tone light. "How did you find out?"

Cole raked his hand through his hair. "One of my employees mentioned that she'd read some coverage online about the Ruby Ball." Cole scowled. "She congratulated me on burying the hatchet with the Musils."

"Nobody was carrying a hatchet at the Ruby Ball, and no one was burying one either."

Cole fixed her with a look she recognized—a lecture from her oldest sibling was coming. "Do I need to remind you about the Musils' reputation?" Not waiting for an answer, he continued, "They've lured away more than one of our employees, tried to use personal connections to try to steal a potential business deal, and basically snuck around until they grew big enough to challenge Serenghetti Construction."

Mia glanced at Jordan—who merely raised his eyebrows—before focusing on Cole again. "Some people would call those tactics good business."

"They were cited for multiple violations on a commercial building job."

She sucked in a breath and then let it out slowly. "Well, that's their problem. What does that have to do with Serenghetti Construction?"

"The Musils targeted us with underhanded tactics. They aimed to succeed by pulling down Serenghetti Construction."

Mia raised her chin. "How do you know?" she

challenged. Only because she wanted the truth, and not to defend Damian, she told herself.

"Listen, Mia, it's a fine line between ethics and corruption, especially in this business," Cole replied. "JM Construction was the winner when the VP of Kenable Management in Springfield was gathering bids for a job. Except now the strip mall exec also has a nice new guest house on his estate that he didn't pay for."

"A kickback or bribe?"

"What do you think?" Cole countered.

Mia threw up her hands.

Jordan cleared his throat. "Face it, Mia. You're not going to convince Cole or the rest of us that the Musils aren't bad news."

Mia rolled her eyes. "Thanks for the verdict."

"Oh, yeah, and you didn't mention Damian the last time I saw you in New York."

"For obvious reasons—"

Jordan nodded.

"—it wasn't any of your business."

Her sister-in-law Marisa walked in, breaking up the battle of words. She held a couple of breadsticks aloft. "Less queasiness this time," she announced, "but I'll be glad when this stage is over."

Cole smiled. "Dahlia is disappointed it's a boy this time."

As Mia widened her eyes, Marisa perched on the arm of an upholstered chair. "We didn't want a big gender reveal party."

Mia's lips twitched. "I'm sure Dahlia will come around."

"She has," her sister-in-law responded, sitting and moving aside a long brown curl that had fallen in front of her amber eyes. "I told her she'll be my helper with the baby while I'm on maternity leave next year."

Mia knew Marisa loved her job as assistant principal at the private school where she'd first met Cole. More importantly, she was glad to have the conversation diverted momentarily from her outing with Damian Musil. "Vincent will be thrilled."

She loved being an aunt to Dahlia, and to Rick and Chiara's son, Vincent. She even dabbled in making clothes for them. She supposed, though, she should thank her lucky stars that Rick, at least, was based in Hollywood and was not around to join the family pile-on today.

A wayward thought popped into her head about what her child and Damian's might look like, and she quickly squelched it. *What was wrong with her?*

Cole raked his hand through his hair again. "Let's get back to the topic at hand."

"Yeah. Damian Musil," Jordan added dryly.

Mia glowered at her youngest brother. "And if I'd mentioned him in New York, what would you have done? Ratted me out to the rest of the family?"

Jordan rubbed his chin. "Tough call."

Sera, Jordan's wife, walked into the room. She was taller than her cousin Marisa and, in contrast, a dark blonde—but the resemblance was there in the amber eyes. She waved a hand as she sat down on a sofa. "I couldn't help overhearing. And no, Jordan, you would have done no such thing. Not if I had anything to say about it."

Mia shot her a look of gratitude. Now that she had three sisters-in-law, she could count on some allies in family squabbles.

"After all," Sera continued as Mia's parents, Camilla and Serg, entered the room, "Mia didn't say a word to anyone when she caught us together in the cloakroom at Oliver's wedding."

All eyes turned to Jordan, who managed to look both sheepish and unapologetic. "Hey, no use upsetting everyone at cousin Oliver's reception with news about my big play."

"Oh, Giordano," Camilla cut in, her words tinged with an Italian accent, "I thought I raised you with better manners."

Jordan gave a lopsided smile. "Sorry, Mom."

Mia kissed her mother in greeting. Although Camilla had learned English at a young age, she still sprinkled her English with Italian. She'd only met her husband when he'd been vacationing in Tuscany and she'd been a twenty-one-year-old hotel front desk employee.

The doorbell rang, and Sera sprang up. "I'll get it."

"You should tell me, *cara*," her mother protested as she sat. "We could pick you up from the bus."

Mia started guiltily. "It wasn't necessary. Really."

"She's got your independent streak, Camilla,"

Serg grumbled as he also accepted Mia's quick peck on the cheek.

As her father took a seat in an armchair near his wife, Mia was glad to see that he seemed in good spirits. Evidently, Cole had not shared the news about Damian Musil with their parents...yet. And her parents' cheer at having family drop by might make the news go over...not catastrophically. At least she hoped so.

Instinctively Mia crossed her fingers behind her back.

She was happy, at least, to see that her father was looking healthy and vigorous—an older version of Cole with steel gray hair mixed with white at the sideburns. After his stroke a few years ago—when he'd stepped back from Serenghetti Construction and handed over the reins to Cole, Serg had fallen into a funk. But these days he was looking more chipper—as if his televised wine spots had injected a new vitality and purpose into his life.

Right when Mia looked away from her parents, however, Sera returned—followed by a familiar face...

Six

"Damian." Mia sucked in a breath. "What are you doing here?"

She drank in the sight of Damian. And then... *Oh, great. Oh, damn.*

Everyone's gaze swung to the entry.

Sera shrugged semi-apologetically. "He said you left something behind."

Cole muttered under his breath. "Musil."

Camilla looked shocked and dismayed, while Serg was patently suspicious.

"Who's going to take the first swing?" Jordan asked no one in particular, his lips twisted into a semblance of the killer smile that had won him underwear billboard ads.

"I'm confused," Serg grumbled.

Confused... Mia thought she could work with merely *confused*.

"And angry. Someone tell me what the hell is going on."

It was all a nightmare. Mia wished the floor would open and swallow her up.

Camilla placed a staying hand on her husband's arm. "Now, Serg."

Her father fixed Mia with a *care to explain* expression. "I may have had a stroke, but I'm understanding this...situation just as much or as little as everyone else."

Before Mia could react, her father turned to Damian. "You've got guts coming here, Musil."

"Compliment accepted, sir," Damian responded easily.

"What are you doing here?" Mia repeated, diverting his attention to her.

She thrummed with awareness. A short time ago, they'd been locked in an embrace. The world had fallen away, and now it was crashing back down on her.

Still, he was so big and calm as he strode over to her, despite the undercurrent of menace in the room. "I wasn't going to let you face your family alone."

"I can fight my own battles," she responded in a low voice.

"Now you don't have to."

"You're complicating things."

"Good."

Cole curled his hands. "Outside, Musil. Now."

"Oh, no, you don't." Mia moved to stand in front of Damian. Even if no punches were thrown, Cole and Jordan together were formidable. In fact, her brothers were all cut from the same cloth—tall, dark...and in excellent physical shape. "We're all staying right here."

"This is a...shock," Camilla remarked faintly.

"Nice to see you, Mrs. Serenghetti," Damian responded. "You're as lovely as your daughter."

Camilla looked flustered and then smiled. "Thank you."

Mia relaxed momentarily. Her mother at least seemed like she was going to maintain at least a semblance of politeness.

"Damn it, Musil," Cole growled, breaking the lull in hostilities. "Save the pretty compliments for the business deals over at JM Construction."

"I don't have anything to do with the construction company these days," Damian said calmly. "My father and brother run it."

"Well, that settles it," Jordan quipped. "In that case, someone invite him to stay for dinner."

Cole snorted. "You're still a Musil—unless you've been disowned?"

"I'm in touch with my family but I run my own business these days."

The understatement of the decade. Mia felt the full impact of what was left unstated. No one in the room needed any primer on how Damian Musil had launched CyberSilver and entered the ranks of the fabulously wealthy.

The tense moment was broken when Dahlia trotted in carrying a toy dump truck.

Spotting Damian, she stopped. "Who are you?"

"Damian Musil."

"I'm Dahlia."

He smiled. "I used to own a truck like that when I was little."

"Figures," Jordan muttered. "Construction is in the blood."

Cole's eyes narrowed. "Dahlia, go play in the rec room again."

The preschooler turned matching hazel eyes on her father. "Daddy, I'm talking to my new person."

Damian crouched and gave the truck a little flick so that it dumped its alphabet block load on the floor.

Dahlia squealed. "Do you want to come play? Daddy does sometimes."

Oh, my heart. Mia felt hers squeeze.

Cole gave an aggrieved sigh. "Dahlia."

Marisa rose and scooped up her daughter with an apologetic look at Damian. "Snack time."

After Marisa had left the room with her daughter, Jordan folded his arms. "You can charm the women in this family, Musil, but we see right through you."

Mia had had enough. "Damian hasn't pulled one over on me."

She'd been back in Welsdale for less than a day and already she seemed to have fallen back into a bad family dynamic—one where everyone thought they knew what was best for her.

On the other hand, she'd be damned if she'd admit

to her family that her relationship with Damian was all a ruse—for the benefit of his business and hers. She was too riled up and annoyed.

"Mia," her father said warningly. "Someone explain to me how you've gotten to know——" he scanned Damian, sizing him up "——this guy."

"He grew up in Welsdale," she said in exasperation, throwing up her hands.

"And somehow, they ended up arm in arm at the Ruby Ball in New York," Cole put in menacingly, locking gazes with Damian.

Camilla's eyes widened while Serg muttered something under his breath—an echo of his eldest son.

"I'd explain," Mia huffed, "but I can see it'd be futile."

Then everyone seemed to be talking at once. Just like the mess of alphabet blocks on the floor, it was chaos...thanks to one deceptively placid-looking tech tycoon.

Mia raised her voice. "Damian and I are leaving. Obviously, no one here is in the mood for a civilized discussion."

As Damian pulled the car away from the Serenghettis' drive, Mia sat next to him in stony silence.

He chanced a glance at her out of the corner of his eye, but she gazed forward unwaveringly.

His arrival at the Serenghettis' had been met with exactly the reaction he'd expected. He'd be damned, though, if he'd let himself be tossed aside because

Mia's family looked down on the Musils—especially after what he and Mia had started in his condo.

He hadn't liked the idea of her showing up and being outnumbered by the rest of her family in an argument. Besides, their underlying beef was with him.

Frankly, he now felt like a knight in shining armor riding off with the damsel in distress—except Mia would eviscerate him for that analogy. He had a car and not a horse, she was a woman who'd proven she could take care of herself, and his armor had a few chinks in it—not least because of his last name, at least as far as the Serenghettis were concerned.

"I can't believe you barged into Serenghetti Central like that," she announced finally, and then turned toward him.

"I didn't barge in," he corrected. "Your sister-in-law opened the door."

"After you misled her with some cooked-up explanation about my leaving something behind."

"You did. Me."

She rolled her eyes. "Yes, thanks for letting everyone know that I had been with you. What were you thinking?"

His hands tightened on the wheel. "I wasn't going to let you face the consequences alone."

"My brothers blowing off steam?" she huffed. "Please, I've dealt with it my whole life."

He bet she had. He and Jordan Serenghetti had crossed paths briefly at Welsdale High School when he'd been a junior and Jordan had nearly been out the door as a senior who was captain of the hockey team. Mia's two older brothers he knew less well. He'd occasionally crossed paths with them in Welsdale, and those interactions could most charitably have been described as an uneasy detente.

A detente that seemed to have ended minutes ago. "I think the correct response is *thank you*."

He knew he'd irritate her, but hey, as long as they were having this out, he was going to defend himself.

"For what?" she huffed. "You gave everyone the impression that something is going on between us. First Carl, now my family."

He took his eyes off the road to glance at her, quirking a brow. "And you didn't contradict the idea."

"This is all business," she responded emphatically.

He didn't say anything but tightened his hands on the wheel again. Mia was deluding herself if she thought that this was only about business. It was about family feuds. It was about a tangled history of decisions overlaid by emotion and distrust. And most of all, it was about the two of them, and the undercurrent of desire running between them.

By the end of their golf outing with the Bensens, Larry had signaled that he would sign a letter of intent to sell his business to Damian, which meant they would be in good faith negotiations to the exclusion of other buyers. The lawyers were going to have to do due diligence, of course, while he and Larry hammered out details, so nothing was sewn up yet. Still, Damian knew he'd taken a major step toward buying Larry's company. Strangely, though, that felt like the least of his concerns right now.

"You act like you're always on a covert mission with your family," he said finally—because he knew better than to voice all his thoughts about the Serenghetti family dynamic he'd witnessed.

"Aren't you with yours? You're the outsider among the Musils, if you're to be believed."

"So we're both rebels with a cause."

She tossed hair away from her face. "Your over-sharing was like throwing oil on the fire for Cole."

He allowed himself a small smile. "Putting a competitor off balance. Good for business."

"Nice try, but you said you're not directly involved with JM Construction—and what were you going to do when the punches started landing?"

"That wasn't going to happen. You jumped in front of me. Who'd have thought a Serenghetti would come to the defense of a Musil?"

"Between you and my brothers, you were the lesser evil."

He gave a short laugh. "Why so caustic when we make each other feel so good?"

She flushed. "Speak for yourself."

He'd been enjoying himself inside his condo until bad news had come barging in. If he could just get to kiss her again—third time was the charm, right? "You were magnificent. You held your own. No need for me to be the heavy, it turns out."

She opened and closed her mouth, seemingly flummoxed and unsure how to react to his words. "I forgot to sew myself a superhero cape."

He arched a brow at her. "You didn't need one. Anyway, aren't you the can-can girl? That costume I liked."

"Of course you did."

He flashed a grin. "For the record, I was on the wrestling team at Welsdale High School. Since then it's been martial arts." He didn't add that he had a black belt. All that focused energy had helped him deal with both his family and his career.

"Cole and Jordan box." It was her turn to raise her eyebrows. "For fun."

"Your brothers may have wanted to hustle me out of the house, but Cole has his business reputation to think about, and Jordan has a public image to maintain, not to mention plenty of endorsement deals. Besides, Dahlia was around. Adorable kid, by the way."

"Someone had to inject some cuteness into the situation."

"We're here," he said with false cheer, pulling into the parking lot beside the luxury condo complex.

A few stray raindrops hit the windshield. *Just in time.*

Mia sighed, and then opened the car door.

"When are we going back to New York?" she asked as she got out.

He followed suit, going around to the trunk for her bag. "Not until morning. Heavy rain and thunderstorms are coming, so we're staying put."

Seven

"What? You can't be serious!" Mia slammed the car door and then looked heavenward. "It doesn't look that bad to me."

Damian held out a hand, and a couple of large drops plopped onto his palm. "Famous last words before the skies open, and all hell breaks loose."

She watched, stupefaction rending her momentarily speechless, while he swung her bag out of the trunk and turned toward the condo complex.

Time to put her foot down, or her umbrella up—maybe both. Was there no end to today's man trouble?

She gesticulated with her hands as she struggled to keep up with him, rain hitting her face and hair with increasing rapidity. "It already poured. At my parents' house when you stormed in. That's why we should head back to New York."

She grabbed the strap of her overnight bag, forcing him to stop. Raindrops had wet his hair. He blinked against a droplet that clung to his eyelashes, and she watched its trajectory as it made its way down to his sensual lips and chiseled jaw.

"There isn't another bus back to New York at this hour from Welsdale, and you know it."

"I'll rent a car then."

"You shouldn't drive back in this weather."

"Fine. I'll go to a hotel." They were toe to toe as they held on to her bag, getting wetter by the second.

"I've got a condo with a guest bedroom."

"Yes, and you come with it."

Damian's lips twitched, and then he leaned toward her so they were nose to nose, too. "What's the matter? Afraid you won't be able to resist me?"

She sucked in a breath, angry and embarrassed. "Oh, puh-leeze."

Still, his words irked her. She didn't like weakness—much less admitting to it. And wasn't Damian only voicing a variation of her brothers' suspicions—that she was in danger of losing her mind over him?

Damian straightened. "Good. Then there's no problem."

Sure, she'd thought back to their kiss at the costume party—their *accidental* kiss. Who wouldn't? It had been embarrassing. *And hot, seductive, pleasurable.* It had made all her dealings with him since then even more fraught.

The fact that the kiss had gone on repeat a short while earlier in his condo, *the one they were walking toward*—well, that was harder to explain away. But she had a long ride back to New York to mull it over—*alone*.

Damian stood like a rock, seemingly oblivious to the rain that continued to hit them. "For a moment there, I thought your opposition to the obvious solution meant—"

"Well, you were wrong."

"Glad that's settled."

She barely had time to process his words before the downpour began in earnest.

Damian cursed, grabbed her hand, and tugged her along.

Together they raced to the overhang sheltering a side entrance of the building.

When they were back inside his condo, they were cold and partly soaked.

Mia shivered and sent droplets flying.

Putting down her bag, Damian reached into a nearby closet and tossed her one of two towels. "Here. Use this."

"Thanks." She rubbed her face and hair, and then realized her white polo top was plastered to her front. Her lacy bra and erect nipples were outlined beneath.

And judging from the direction of Damian's stare, he'd noticed, too.

Her gaze traveled to his chest with its clearly defined muscles... She hugged the towel to her front.

He jerked his head toward the interior of the condo. "The guest bedroom is back there if you want to change."

"Thanks." She grabbed her bag and strode forward, intent on putting some distance between herself and Damian—and regrouping.

No way was she staying. Unfortunately for her, though, the torrential downpour continued unabated while she changed into drier clothes—sweats—and freshened up in the bathroom across the hall.

She was caught between a rock and a hard place. If she continued to insist on leaving, she'd seem mulish and put the lie to her denial that being alone with him…what? Made her aware of herself as a woman? She wouldn't give him the satisfaction. On the other hand, if she stayed, something *might* happen…

C'mon, Mia. You've dealt with more distracting situations than this one. She could trust herself… couldn't she?

When she wandered back to the front of the condo, she found Damian in the kitchen, contemplating the food arrayed on the counter before him.

She braced herself for some smugness or an I-told-you-so, but instead he gave her an apologetic look.

He gestured at the spread he'd laid out. "I don't stay here often, so it looks like our choice is mostly frozen pizza and hard seltzer."

She resolved to be gracious in her discomfiture. "Sounds exactly like what I was thinking."

While his hair was still damp, he'd changed into a T-shirt and jeans.

"Meaning you pegged me for the type to have an empty fridge with nothing but a container of leftover takeout?" he asked drolly.

Rather than answering, she moved closer to peer at the pizza box. "Feta, pineapple and pepperoni?"

"You've never tried it?" he said, feigning surprise.

"I'm more of a spinach and artichoke type. But I'm sure it's...delicious."

Damian lifted the side of his mouth. "Trust me."

Wasn't that the issue?

Her gaze skittered away from his, and she busied herself opening a can of wild cherry seltzer.

She focused on setting the table while he heated the pizza. Afterward, she made a pretense of scrolling through work emails on her phone while they waited for the food to be ready. Anything to distract herself from Damian moving around casually in the kitchen nearby.

When they finally sat down at the small dining table to eat, Mia took some bites of food and found herself unexpectedly relaxing. She'd been hungrier than she'd thought.

Damian eyed her plate. "Looks as if you like that pepperoni, pineapple and feta pizza after all."

She swallowed and dabbed at her mouth with a napkin. "Surprisingly good."

"See, try something new and—"

"The correct response is *thank you*?" she parried, echoing his words earlier.

He gave her a lopsided smile. "Sorry I couldn't deliver anything close to the home-cooked meal that you'd have gotten at your parents' house."

Struck by his unexpected apology, she found herself wanting to reassure him. "Yes, but then I would have had to deal with my relatives, and as you could tell, families can be difficult sometimes. It's like you're slotted into a role and typecast. At least that's how I feel."

Damian quirked his lips. "That's what happens with people who've known you for a long time."

She took a sip of her drink. "Please don't claim to be a rebel again. I think I've got that role locked up. Anyway, from all appearances, you're the American dream personified. The son of immigrants who climbed to the gazillionaire ranks."

"Yeah, but when you're an immigrant, family loyalty usually counts for more. In Jakob Musil's eyes, I should have stayed in Welsdale to raise JM Construction to new heights."

She could tell him a thing or two about family loyalty, too.

He leaned back in his chair. "And after my mother died, the family got even tighter. It was just me, my brother and my dad."

"I'm sorry." She knew that Damian's mother had died suddenly when he was thirteen. She'd been ten at the time but she'd heard people in town mentioning it.

Damian shrugged. "It was a long time ago."

"But the scar is still there." She didn't know why

she made the comment—only that something in his eyes had belied his casual words.

"The scar is what made me who I am today. Though I don't think Dad understood it."

She tilted her head inquiringly.

"I fast-tracked my life. Not just to get away from the sadness at home, but because I got a firsthand look at the cliché that life is short. After she died, I let ambition fuel me."

Ambition was *her* fuel, too, but what a terrible thing to have it lit by the death of a parent.

"So I powered through Carnegie Mellon in five years for a joint computer science and MBA degree."

"And the rest is history," she said half-jokingly.

He arched a brow. "Only if you read the business press."

"You're not doing too shabbily on the New York social scene, either."

"Obviously," he deadpanned. "I showed up at the Ruby Ball with Mia Serenghetti as my date."

She flushed.

Did she want these insights into Damian Musil? It was so much easier to treat him as a two-dimensional character—a villain with sex appeal.

Mia curled up in a corner of the overstuffed sofa—and nursed her cup of chamomile. Outside the driving rain pounded against the Juliet balcony even though the hour already neared midnight. She saw a flash of lightning, and moments later, it was accompanied by claps of thunder.

She hadn't been able to sleep, even though it had been a long day. The Bensens were lovely people, but she'd still been unable to relax completely during the golf game. Not when she was aware of Damian's every move. At one point, she'd caught Allison giving her a knowing look. Who'd have thought that a Serenghetti and a Musil would ever be on the same team?

And then, of course, Damian had shocked her by turning up at her parents' house. He truly believed he'd come to her defense, and she in turn had jumped in to defend him. Now everyone thought they really were a couple.

"I thought I heard noise."

Mia jerked with surprise, and then put her sloshing mug down on an end table.

Damian stood silhouetted in the doorway. He was bare chested, and sweats hung low on his hips. If she'd thought he'd emanated sex appeal in jeans and a T-shirt, she was in no way prepared for the sight of a seminude Damian, his hair tousled from bed.

In the dim lighting afforded by a small lamp, Mia traced the lines of sculpted muscle—hard biceps, flat abs, ripped pecs. He worked out—*obviously*. And his stint on the wrestling team and his martial arts training didn't hurt.

When Damian's lips twitched, she averted her gaze. *Don't touch.* As long as there was no contact, she'd be fine…

He sauntered forward and sat down next to her.

"Sorry if I woke you," she mumbled.

"I had a hard time sleeping, too."

She was curled up, but Damian sprawled—his arm resting on the back of the sofa.

Her resolution about touching was getting harder to keep by the second. *Damn it.* Was he testing her? But no—he looked like the personification of ease while she verged on painful awareness.

"The thunder could wake anybody," he commented.

You could wake anyone. While she'd struggled to sleep in the guest bedroom, she'd been aware of Damian beyond the bedroom wall in the next room. Her thoughts had hopped and skipped around, but Damian had been like a low hum in the back of her mind.

"What have you been thinking?"

She flushed. "Just contemplating the rain."

"Did storms bother you when you were a kid?"

"Not really."

"I guess there's no chance of you jumping into my arms with fright?" he teased.

She straightened on the sofa, uncurling her legs and planting her feet on the floor. "In your dreams."

He tilted his head. "I can almost taste you there, you know."

She gave a strained laugh. "Those must be some vivid dreams."

"Very."

A shiver of awareness chased down her spine, and she tingled all over.

"Do you want details?" His voice was low, intimate.

"What flavor am I?" she asked, her voice hitching.

No touching, no touching, no touching. She hung on to that resolution like a lifeline.

He quirked his lips. "What part of you am I sampling?"

Wow. Erotic images flashed through her mind. "Are you trying to seduce me?"

He reached for her hand and kissed the back of it. "You have no problems resisting me, remember?"

She sucked in a breath. "Right."

She'd resolved not to make the first move, but she searched her muddled mind about what was supposed to happen if *he* did.

"On the other hand, I want you badly."

"Oh." She wanted to ask since when—

"Your brothers saw right through me. Your family doesn't like it."

She drew in an offended breath. "Who cares?"

She stared at his lips, the plains of his chest visible in the semidarkness and then thrown into relief by a flash of lightning. She lifted her gaze and met his.

It was like he was willing her to make a move—coaxing her to touch him. The tension radiated from him like heat from a bonfire. Too bad the rain was outside and couldn't douse the flames licking her right now.

She wet her lips, and he made a sound.

Honestly, it was hard to hold on to the idea of

him as the bad guy. *It was hard to think at all.* He'd walked right into the firestorm at her parents' house—and, traitorously, she'd momentarily thrilled at the sight of him after the initial shock. The whole situation had tested her loyalties, confusing her with her impulse to guard him from her family.

He was a Musil, but she'd started thinking of him as just Damian. Friend or enemy—or something else?

"I have no trouble resisting you." The words rang hollow even to her own ears.

"Ah. Yeah. But we didn't say anything about my resisting you."

If he'd touched her first, did that mean her own resolution about touching no longer applied? Plus, he'd found the weak chink in her armor by mentioning her family. She had a long insubordinate streak.

Slipping her hand over his shoulder, she exerted gentle pressure and brought his head forward.

"One last act of rebellion by getting it on with a Musil?" he muttered.

"Why not?" she whispered against his lips. "Everyone thinks I already have."

He groaned.

And then their lips touched, in a kiss that was hot and full of promise.

Damian angled her head and leisurely explored her mouth. She met him caress for caress as the kiss deepened. When he sought more, she tipped back and he leaned forward. And then he was bringing her legs onto his lap and following her down until her head rested on the arm of the sofa.

Still holding the kiss, he pushed back the gaping top of her pajama shirt.

Mia arched her back, her nipples brushing his chest and hardening. She shifted, seeking his touch, her body humming. Her pulse thrummed through her, hot and heavy with excitement…anticipation.

Damian fisted his hand in her shirt and pulled it down to expose her shoulder and the top of her breast. Then he trailed his lips along her jaw and down the side of her neck, pausing to nip her shoulder before stroking featherlight kisses on her breast.

"Do you always wander around the house without your shirt on?" she managed on a sigh.

He gave a low chuckle. "Hey, at least I put on my sweats before coming out here. I didn't want to scandalize you."

"We've been building to a scandal for weeks."

"Why stop now?" he murmured.

It was hard to come up with an answer.

And then his mouth was on her breast, and Mia forgot to think at all. Instead, she threaded her fingers through his hair and gave herself up to the sensation of Damian lavishing attention on the soft mound.

Sensation shot through her and pooled between her legs.

He moved to her other breast, and she whimpered.

"Mia," he said hoarsely when he lifted his head

moments later. "You're even more spectacular than I imagined."

She breathed in deep. "What do I taste like?"

His eyes glittered in a flash of lightning. "Like heaven."

She pulled his head down for a lingering kiss until they were a tangle of limbs. His erection brushed against her, evidence that he was aroused.

When the kiss finally ended, he leveraged himself up and stood. Before she could react, he lifted her into his arms and she squeaked.

Instinctively, she linked her arms around his neck to anchor herself, and Damian strode across the room. Thunder rumbled outside and the rain came down with renewed fury.

"Is this to demonstrate how strong you are?" she teased weakly, adjusting to the unaccustomed sensation of being carried—literally swept off her feet. "I believed you about the martial arts and the rest, you know."

Damian kicked open his bedroom door. "This has nothing to do with showing off. I'm desperate, and I have protection in my room. Or at least I hope to hell I do."

Peripherally, Mia took note of the masculine bedroom done in muted neutrals that she'd glimpsed earlier through the partially open door. And then she found herself deposited on the rumpled king-size bed.

With a couple of fluid moves, Damian opened a

small zippered travel pouch on the night table and placed a foil packet on the polished wood.

She raised herself on her elbows and glanced around at the tangle of sheets. "Looks like you were having a rough night."

"You have no idea." He began stripping off his sweats.

Dear sweet fashion gods. "You don't need clothes."

"Afraid I'll put you out of business?" he teased.

She flushed.

"Yeah, I don't need clothes, I need you. Now."

Yes.

He clamped a hand on her ankle and pulled her toward him while she gave a small exclamation. When he stripped the sweatpants from her, he paused appreciatively. "Red panties."

She heated. "I was in a hurry and tossed them when I was changing."

He started unbuttoning her flannel shirt the rest of the way—and then fumbled.

His impatience—she'd never call Damian nervous—excited her further.

"Here let me."

While she worked at the buttons, he slid his hands up her legs and under her butt, and then trailed his lips up her inner thigh.

"Let's get these silky red panties off you."

She squirmed, and then his mouth found her hot core and she gasped.

With relief, she slid her arms out of her shirt sleeves and tugged him toward her.

"What do you want, Mia?" he breathed against her mouth.

"You. I want you."

They couldn't move fast enough then. He tossed the last pieces of clothing from the bed, and they were a tangle of limbs when thunder rumbled again. He touched her everywhere, arousing her with his mouth and hands.

Somehow they ended up switching positions, and she was on top, astride him. She caressed his length, aching to touch him, and watched him from under lowered lashes.

He closed his eyes on a hiss.

"Yes?"

"Mia."

She tasted him with her mouth, and his hand tangled in her hair.

Damian groaned but held still. "Sweet."

He jerked beneath her attentions, and his free hand fisted in the sheets.

When she sensed that he was on the brink, she straightened, brushed her hair aside, and rolled protection onto his length. She leaned down to kiss him again, and he surprised her by flipping her onto her back one more time.

Testing first, he then entered her in one fluid motion, and they both moaned.

Damian muttered something unintelligible against her neck. Moments later, he started moving, setting a tempo that she met with a counterpoint.

With the storm raging outside, Damian's arms

seemed both the safer and more dangerous place to be. He adjusted her hips and suddenly he was hitting her in the exact right spot.

"Oh." Her breath came in gasps.

"Let it happen, Mia," he groaned into her ear. "Come for me."

It was the last encouragement she needed. She spasmed, her hips undulating against him and setting off his own orgasm.

They clung together, waves of sensation lifting them higher until they finally ebbed away, leaving them panting.

Moments later, Damian rolled off her and covered his eyes with his arm. "I went to heaven."

She giggled. "Better than your fantasies?"

Damian turned toward her and propped himself on an elbow. "Yup, and there were plenty of those."

He traced a finger down her chest between her breasts. "I used to wonder what the girl with the flashing eyes was thinking."

"Please, you hardly noticed me."

"I did," he insisted.

"I was a lowly freshman when you were a senior at Welsdale High."

"Remember Jacinda's pool party? I could barely take my eyes off you."

She recalled surreptitiously checking him out, too. "I remember shopping around for the perfect retro swimsuit."

"One that accented your curves."

He circled a finger around her breast, and her eyelids fluttered.

"One that flattered my coloring."

"If you say so."

"Mmm." She sighed languorously, and then turned her head when a glint of gold on the night table caught her attention. "You wear jewelry?"

She didn't recall Damian ever sporting any—not even a watch.

"It's a keepsake that I sometimes travel with." He paused and scanned her gaze. "A chain necklace that my mother bought when I was born."

"Ah. She's still part of who you are."

"Yes."

She was startled by the insight. Another sign that she was failing badly at keeping her distance from Damian. He'd even melted her heart by his interaction with Dahlia, in the midst of a charged conversation with the rest of her family.

She and Damian had kept their distance from each other over the years. Their families' rivalry had been like an insurmountable wall even in the face of any stirrings of attraction. But now that wall was crumbling. Her heart pounded. They'd dated, they'd kissed, they'd gotten to know each other better and realize how much they had in common... *They'd just had sex.* Wow, she was in deep...

Eight

The next morning, Damian woke to find Mia already gone from his bed. Then he realized the water was running in the guest bath. He was semi-aroused and disappointment that she wasn't still in bed with him washed away the remnants of sleep.

Turning his head, he saw the bedside clock said it wasn't even half past seven. He hadn't slept in—she'd gotten up early. With a mental shrug, he figured that maybe Mia was one of those women who didn't want to be seen first thing in the morning. She didn't strike him as the type, but then again, she was in the fashion business, where appearances were everything.

Settling back against the pillow, he stretched and folded his arms behind his head. It had been damn good between them last night. And if she'd still been tucked around him this morning, he'd have picked up where they'd left off.

He and Mia had slept together. His life had been one rapid climb, and yesterday he'd reached new heights.

He'd also faced the Serenghettis without getting ruffled...if you didn't count falling in lust with the firebrand of the family. Oh, yeah, he'd known he'd had a weakness. But he hadn't realized that getting closer to her would *increase* the pull of attraction instead of satisfying it once and for all. His past relationships had all been short-term. He'd been far more focused on the demands of his start-up business.

Instead, yesterday, he hadn't been so concerned about the satisfaction of having the Serenghettis face a Musil who'd legitimately grown more successful than they were as he'd been ready to defend Mia.

Crap, things couldn't get any more complicated. He was known for his cool unflappability in the boardroom—he'd counted on it carrying him through a mutually beneficial arrangement with Mia Serenghetti. Instead, he'd gotten more than he bargained for. More than a taste...more than a fleeting flirtation...more everything.

And he wanted more.

With a grunt of sexual frustration, he lowered his arms and threw back the sheets. He showered, dressed, and headed to the kitchen to make breakfast and answer some work emails.

When Mia appeared, she was wearing a yellow jumpsuit that wasn't revealing but nonetheless hugged her curves. She was like the sun emerging after a storm.

He felt a kick of lust and reined in his desire. He nodded apologetically at the food arrayed in front of him. "From frozen."

"I'm sure it's delicious," she responded brightly.

He'd rather feast on her. He eyed the overnight bag that she'd brought out with her. "In a hurry?"

"I wanted to be packed and ready to go," she said, flushing but setting down the bag. "I wasn't just taking my time to primp…in case you were wondering."

"Now why would I think that," he drawled, "when you're a fashion superstar?"

"Aspiring."

"You have to dream it before you live it."

She came closer and picked up an empty mug. "That's your mantra, huh?"

He poured some coffee while she breathed in the aroma and smiled appreciatively. "It worked out okay."

They stood at the kitchen counter and bit into the egg sandwiches he'd made. Sunlight shafted through the windows and onto the sofa in the nearby living room.

He watched the rays of light add to her luminescence. "The rain stopped, but it's still wet out."

"Mmm," she replied absently, and then swallowed.

Damian reached up and swiped the corner of her mouth with his thumb. "Crumb."

She stilled, and he brushed her lips with his.

"There, all better."

"Don't assume this means more than it does," she said after an awkward silence.

"What?" he joked. "Removing a speck of food from your lips?"

"You know what I mean."

"Isn't that usually the guy's line? No strings?"

She rolled her eyes. "It happened."

He smiled wolfishly. "It was good."

"I'm not into casual hookups—"

"Neither am I."

"I'm too busy with my career."

"Of course."

"But I'm a mature adult, so I know these things happen. We scratched that itch."

"What about if we want to do it again?"

"I don't respond to booty calls."

"Actually I prefer to text," he teased.

She sighed impatiently.

"Okay, what about a date?"

She widened her eyes. "Us? No, forget it."

"Why not?"

"You know why not, and it starts with our last names."

He thought fast. "The Bensens think we're a couple, so we need to play this one out."

"Until you get your business deal—"

"And you have a firm contact in Katie."

She looked momentarily disappointed. "Right."

"C'mon, you wouldn't want Carl to think that

I was only a quick rebound relationship," he said half-jokingly. "Right now, he thinks you've moved on with his former boss. You're golden."

For some reason, the thought didn't seem to cheer her up.

"And let's not forget why we fell into bed." He lifted the side of his mouth.

"The storm—"

"Your rebellious streak. Face it, I'm your biggest rebellion yet."

"I'm more clearheaded this morning."

"Still gorgeous, though."

"My designs are meant to bring out the best in a woman."

Taking a sip of his coffee, he said, "Yeah, I figured the sexy jumpsuit was one of your own creations."

She wet her lips, but then took a step back, as if she didn't trust herself—them—not to speed back up the wrong ramp right now.

He sobered. "I've got a quick stop to make before we hit the road to New York."

She tilted her head.

"JM Construction. My father asked me to drop by, and—" he shrugged "—his office is on the road back to New York."

Her eyes widened, and then she shrugged. "We already had our moment with the Serenghettis, so I guess that's fair."

"A Serenghetti arguing to be fair to the Musils?" he murmured. "Never say never."

She raised her eyebrows at him before taking another sip of coffee.

Twenty minutes later, they made their way across the parking lot to his car.

Damian watched Mia sidestep a puddle. Then he opened the trunk and placed their bags inside. "It might be an extended conversation so you may want to come inside with me."

She adjusted the sunglasses perched on her head. "I guess you'll be protecting me from *your* big bad family this time."

Damian bit back a laugh. But damn it—why did the Serenghetti-Musil competition have to rear its head again right now? He didn't see the competition to buy the same construction company ending well. "You won't need protecting."

"Because I'm a badass?" she asked.

He snapped the trunk shut. "Yeah, and they'll be too busy gunning for me."

Her eyes widened. "You're the outlaw in a renegade clan?"

"Do two negatives cancel each other out?" he parried, searching her gaze. "Would that make me a paragon?"

"We'll see," she responded, giving him an oblique look. "Anyway, with a Serenghetti on the premises, won't they be worried about, you know, corporate espionage…?"

He smiled slightly. "Come on. You can judge for yourself."

***

JM Construction was located in a nondescript commercial strip on one of the main roads leading out of Welsdale. Mia had driven by it plenty of times as a teen without giving it too much attention—except to occasionally wonder whether Damian was there.

He'd sometimes worked a summer job for the family business like her brothers did for Serenghetti Construction. One episode in particular was imprinted on her memory. She'd been heading to a frozen yogurt store to meet up with a couple of high school girlfriends. Damian had been hauling equipment out of the back of a pickup. Their gazes had collided—he'd given her a quick sweeping look, a slight nod of the head, and then an almost imperceptible smile. She'd swept her hair off her shoulder and walked on, pretending she hadn't noticed. Inside she'd sizzled. *With annoyance.* Or so she'd told herself.

He should have known that if he so much as looked in her direction, her brothers would pounce. And yet, years later, it hadn't stopped him...

They'd spent the whole night together. She'd woken twice in the middle of the night—once to find Damian's arm draped over her, and later, to find herself snuggled against him. When the sun had come up, she'd woken first and tiptoed back to the guest bedroom for a shower and to get ready—and to collect her thoughts.

Musils and Serenghettis did not date. Or have sex.

She and Damian had simply entered a mutually advantageous agreement that had gotten complicated. But there was still time to get on the right track.

This was business. She kicked a pebble as they walked to the front door of JM Construction.

Moments later, Mia surveyed her surroundings. The office manager was busy on the phone, an employee in work boots was exiting via a side door and voices could be heard in the back office.

It was all rather mundane. Rather like Serenghetti Construction, actually—or rather what she remembered her family business being while she was growing up. The Musils' company, on the other hand, clearly remained small and scrappy—an opponent nipping at the heels.

Mia wasn't sure what she should have been expecting. Maybe something more ominous and forbidding. Darth Vader's theme song playing in the background, perhaps.

Damian gestured for her to follow him and they turned a corner to the back offices.

She recognized Jakob Musil instantly. An older version of Damian, he was standing in the hall talking to a younger man. His companion turned, and Mia recognized Valentin, Damian's younger brother. He'd still been in middle school when she'd crossed paths with Damian at Welsdale High.

"Damian, you're finally here." Jakob's voice was gruff but his perusal was a tad quizzical.

"Dad, this is Mia Serenghetti," Damian said,

seeming to shrug off any implicit criticism in his father's greeting.

Mia steeled herself, but if they were shocked or surprised, neither Jakob nor Valentin showed it.

Instead, Jakob looked at her shrewdly for a couple of moments. "Ah, Mia Serenghetti. I remember when you were—"

He gestured with his hand to indicate a height under five feet.

Mia drew herself up. She might not match her brothers' or Damian's six-foot frames, but at five-seven, she thought she held her own these days. "Nice to see you, Mr. Musil."

Jakob nodded his head. "Perhaps you've come as the family emissary ready to negotiate about the competition to buy Tevil Construction?"

"I know nothing about it, Mr. Musil," Mia responded. "The family construction company is my brother Cole's business to run these days."

Thanks to Jordan, she knew that Tevil Construction was the latest flashpoint between the Musils and Serenghettis. Well, except for the matter of her and Damian and their little arrangement...

"But you are still a Serenghetti, yes? And Serg's daughter."

"Yes, but—"

"Dad, Mia is here because we were invited to play a game of golf yesterday with another couple."

"Interesting," Valentin commented, finally speaking up.

"We were asked to make up a pair for golf," Mia

added quickly, and then shrugged. "You know, so much business happens on the golf course…"

Not a couple, not a couple. Not in a real sense.

Damian shot her an amused look, and she pursed her lips.

What was wrong with him? The false advertising about their fake relationship was gaining a wider audience, day by day. At this rate, he should go ahead and take out a billboard in Times Square.

Perplexed, Jakob looked at her. "So you and my son are on the same team?"

"Not exactly."

Valentin quirked a brow. "Yeah, because who'd believe a Musil—"

Damian shot his brother a quelling look.

"It was a business outing," Mia offered lamely.

Valentin shrugged. "Right. Because we know Damian isn't in your league."

Mia heated and bit the inside of her cheek. Was Valentin suggesting that Damian wasn't good enough for her—or vice versa?

"Damian isn't in *our* league anymore, either," Jakob observed.

Well, that certainly cleared things up for her.

Damian's expression grew tense. "Dad—"

"Why else do you come back so little? That condo of yours is gathering dust."

Not last night.

Still, Mia felt a jolt and an inexplicable urge to defend Damian. After all, she could relate—to being overscheduled with a career and not wanting to fall back into a discouraging family dynamic, and for so many other reasons. But she clamped her mouth shut.

"I've been busy," Damian said without inflection.

"Yes, with the new Musil empire." Jakob looked around. "What was wrong with building on what's here?"

"We could use your fancy business degree," Valentin added dryly.

Mia glanced around at her surroundings again. They were bare bones, especially in comparison to Cole's glossy headquarters in Welsdale these days. But JM Construction would always be the upstart nipping at Serenghetti Construction's heels.

"Dad, construction was never my thing even though I worked plenty of summers here."

"Construction too old-fashioned for you? Working with your hands and getting dirty?"

Mia shifted uncomfortably. This was fast becoming an argument. Sort of like a mirror of her family, except she had no trouble mouthing off when it was another Serenghetti.

Damian sighed, as if this was a conversation he'd had before. "It wasn't that."

"How many generations does it take to wash the dirty money, eh?" Jakob mused, almost to himself.

Damian said nothing but a muscle ticked in his jaw.

Mia wanted to disappear but she was also transfixed.

"Just remember—" Jakob nodded at his surroundings "—this business paid the bills for your education."

Damian raked his hand through his hair.

Jakob turned to her. "What do you think?"

What? "I—"

"Let's leave Mia out of this."

"Why? She's obviously important if you brought her here."

Was no one listening to her protestations about a meaningless golf game?

"And she's also a Serenghetti. I'm sure she has strong opinions," Jakob added.

"Seems like we're going to retrace old ground," Damian muttered. "All of it."

Mia splayed her hands. "To be truthful, I went off to work in New York, too. I'm...biased."

"But you get home to visit?" Jakob pressed.

Yup, like yesterday—much to her regret. "Well, I—"

Jakob chuckled. "And you don't hold any animosity toward us Musils. Because you're not involved with Serenghetti Construction—" he gestured toward Damian "—but you are with my son." Jakob looked slyly between Damian and Mia. "Golf game, yes?"

"Well, to be fair, I do know that you and my family have some history."

Jakob lowered his brows at her words. "What history?"

"The incident with the Kenable exec, Dad," Damian said, breaking in. "Let's start there, since we're rehashing things."

"What about it?" Jakob shot back, lowering his brows at Damian.

Mia was familiar with that look. She'd seen it on… Serg Serenghetti. She wondered what her father would think about the similarity to his rival and erstwhile nemesis.

Valentin sighed and leaned his shoulder against the hallway wall. "Here we go."

"Dad, he got a free guest house," Damian said.

"Only after he was not employed by the shopping mall developer anymore."

"But you discussed it with him before you got the contract."

"It came up in conversation. But why does it matter?" Jakob said impatiently. "JM Construction was the best for the job."

"And he got a new guest residence for giving you the business."

Mia supposed an underdog had to do what an underdog had to do. Didn't she know that herself these days, trying to break into the big time in the fashion business?

Jakob shook his head. "No, he paid for the raw materials, and we supplied labor for the guest house. It was a small project, and now he's a friend. What's wrong with doing a favor for a friend?"

Damian sighed. "Dad, we've been at an impasse on this issue for years. Let's just agree to disagree."

Suddenly, Jakob's shoulders lowered. "You think it's easy struggling with a new business and a young family? Then I lost my wife. I did what I had to do to survive… Maybe I would not make the same decision again."

Mia flushed and her heart squeezed. "Mr. Musil, I understand."

All three men stilled and looked at her. She wasn't sure who was most surprised.

"You do, eh?" Jakob finally asked.

"Yes. Sometimes it's not the facts but how we choose to interpret them—and our options—at the time." Her brother's indictment of the Musils had seemed damning. Maybe JM Construction had made a few missteps, particularly in its earlier days, but companies changed. People could change.

She understood—she was trying to build her own brand. She'd always striven to be ethical, but competition was stiff, like in every other business. And temptation could be lurking right around the next corner.

Damian's father relaxed a bit. "It's Jakob. And explain that to your brother Cole."

"I can't. We're not exactly on great terms right now."

Jakob looked between her and his son, a perceptive twinkle in his eye. "I don't ask why."

Damian muttered something, but it seemed as if the tension had broken.

"It's a little late in the game, but why did you want me to stop by, Dad?" Damian asked, his tone holding a note of forbearance.

Jakob suddenly chuckled and lightened. "Yes, I have something to give you." His gaze drifted to Mia. "And looks like the timing may be good."

They all followed him into the nearest office,

which was sparsely furnished with a metal desk, two chairs and file cabinets.

Jakob picked up a small red box and held it out to Damian. "Here. Your mother wanted you to have this. Some of her personal possessions that she wanted divided between you and your brother by the time that you were both thirty. You weren't in Welsdale for Valentin's last birthday, so I'm doing it while I know you are here. This one's yours."

Damian took the box slowly. "Thanks."

Jakob nodded. "You don't have to open it now."

Damian rubbed the back of his neck. "Yup, I think Mia has seen enough drama."

All weekend. Mia took a deep breath. First her family, then the Musils, and she wasn't even counting the little interlude with Damian in between.

Dear sweet heaven, she'd slept with the enemy—and now she was having trouble remembering that's what he was supposed to be.

Things happened quickly after that. Jakob invited them to stay for coffee, and she quickly learned that for all the awkwardness and roughness, the Musils were bound by loss and a deep history. Jakob and Valentin were soon called away by business, however, and Damian announced that he and Mia needed to get on the road.

That's when Mia was brought back to the realization that she still had a long drive back to New York in close quarters with Damian…

Nine

"Well, that went well," Damian remarked dryly as soon as he and Mia were on the road again.

"Hmm."

He glanced at her out of the corner of his eye. "Hmm?"

"I've never been inside JM Construction before."

He laughed. "I didn't think so, even though you had a reputation for being rebellious back in high school."

She turned her head toward him. "Meaning I might have broken in?"

"I said rebel, not spy. That wouldn't have fit the role."

"And what tipped you off? The purple hair? The nose ring?"

His lips twitched. "Yeah, what happened to that ring?"

She folded her arms. "I got bored with the experiment, and the hole closed by itself."

He chanced another glance at her. "You mean you'd achieved your goal of shocking your family, and it was time to move on."

She swept him with a look of mock affront. "You think so, Mr. Straight-and-Narrow?"

"Hardly."

She gestured at him. "Look at you. So clean-cut, there's barely a swerve to you."

"Meaning I had no surprise moves last night?" he parried.

She sucked in a breath.

"I love it when you get all bothered over me," he teased, before adopting a thoughtful expression. "You know, it surprised me when you went into fashion."

"Because of what I was like in high school?"

He nodded.

"It's not that surprising," she sniffed. "I have two aunts on my mother's side who were talented seamstresses before they sold their shop and retired. I spent a couple of summers with them in Italy, sort of apprenticing."

"Ah, no wonder I didn't see you in a new bikini every season."

She tossed him a quelling look. "Lots of Serenghettis are creative types. Even construction is an art form if you think about it."

"So I suppose that explains why you came to my

father's defense back there. One artist backing another."

She opened and closed her mouth. "I wasn't choosing sides, just trying to see both."

He quirked a brow at her.

She glanced out the window. "My family doesn't like that JM Construction hired away some of their employees, but there's nothing illegal about it. And every construction company has run afoul of complicated codes over the years. With any luck, they weren't serious violations, and they've learned from them. Every company also tries to attract new business. As far as Kenable, though, your father admitted he might not make the same business decision today."

"Says the entrepreneur."

She tossed her hair. "Whatever. But yes, I've got some insight now that I'm running my own company."

"Naturally."

"You know, that was the first time he said that he might have made a mistake. Maybe it was the occasion of passing along heirlooms. Or maybe...it was because you were there."

She flushed.

He liked that Mia had warmed to his family. He also liked that she didn't think of his father as just another wrongdoer. Damn it, he liked *her*.

She shifted in her seat, as if uncomfortable with her own admissions. "Do you mind if we play some music?"

"That depends," he teased.

"On what?"

"Your musical tastes."

"You're impossible," she said, leaning forward and fiddling with the car stereo.

When she glanced out the window again, he caught the faint sounds of classic rock. They settled into a companionable silence, and he took the curves of the open road that wound between rolling hills.

She seemed lost in a reverie but eventually started mouthing some lyrics. Soon, to his amusement, the mouthing turned into humming and then singing under her breath.

"Caterwauling?" he commented.

She turned toward him. "What?"

"Do you always sing in the car?"

"Are you saying you don't like my voice?"

"I like it." He'd *dreamed* about it.

She tossed him a quizzical look. "I get the singing from my mother. She loves musicals. In fact, she named Cole after Cole Porter."

Damian rubbed his jaw thoughtfully, thinking it had escaped without even a punch yesterday. "Your brother lived up to his eloquent namesake yesterday. His words were music to my ears."

Mia tried and failed to suppress a smile.

"I should have guessed you took after your mother. Even aside from being beautiful, you also like music."

Mia grew flustered and glanced out at the passing landscape.

They drove in silence except for the low music, and the next time Damian glanced over at her, he was surprised to find that her eyes had fluttered shut. She'd dozed off.

A feeling suspiciously like tenderness swept over him. This weekend had tired her out. When he reached Manhattan, though, he knew he needed to rouse her because they would soon be at her place.

He turned up the volume and started crooning along to "My Girl."

Within minutes, Mia blinked and opened her eyes. Stretching, she asked, "What's that caterwauling?"

Damian laughed. "That's my girl…"

She rolled her eyes.

"What, you don't like the song? You know, we are in May, and you are—"

"Not sunshine. Please." She looked pained at his reference to the lyrics.

He grinned.

"You know, your singing voice isn't half bad," she sniffed.

"You should hear me in the shower," he purred.

"Caterwauling at the break of dawn."

He chuckled. "I'm not familiar with that song."

"Of course not."

When he pulled up in front of her building, there wasn't a parking spot in sight. *Damn it.* If they'd been at his place, he could have tossed the car keys to a doorman. But she lived in a walkup above her studio, in what looked like a renovated tenement on a side street in the Garment District. That much he'd established when he'd picked her up for the Ruby Ball—what seemed like eons ago.

Before their world had shifted. Before they'd hooked up. Before he'd met her family and she'd met his. Before she'd had his back, and he'd had hers, and they'd had each other…

She turned to look at him. "Thanks for the ride."

He nodded, flexing his hands on the steering wheel. Because otherwise it would be too tempting to reignite the passion between them, even with the passing pedestrians offering no privacy.

"I'd better get out before you, you know, get a ticket."

Nodding, he got out along with her. He was pulled up alongside some parked cars, and traffic continued to plow by on his driver's side.

After opening the trunk, he passed the overnight bag to her.

When their hands brushed, she stilled, and he quirked a knowing brow.

Her phone buzzed, and shifting, she fished it out of her handbag with her free hand. She frowned down at the screen for a moment. "I'd better get this. Work calls."

Text me. Call me. Sleep with me. But he said none of those things.

Instead, he shoved his hands in his pockets and watched her walk into her building.

But not out of his life.

They needed to see their arrangement through

as far as the Bensons and their daughter were concerned.

And hell if he'd let himself be ghosted.

"I'm worried about you, *cara*."

"Stop, Mom. I'm fine. Really." Mia paced inside her work studio. The late afternoon sun filtered weakly through the security bars on the back windows, little particles of dust floating in the beams of light.

"I don't know... You don't seem yourself."

Mia blew out a breath. In other words, *let's talk about the kerfuffle that happened in Welsdale this weekend with Damian Musil.*

"Should I come down to New York to see you?"

Ack. No. It was enough trouble when her brothers dropped into the city. Mia absently twisted the tie on her denim jumpsuit.

Next time, she thought absently, she'd add a hidden cinch waist. She was always searching for ways to make her next design better...

"We could get reservations at a nice restaurant. There's a new place—"

"Mom, everything is okay." She'd gone restaurant hopping with her mother in the past, but right now the last thing Mia needed was for her mother to come to New York.

"Are you sure?"

Mia sighed. "You're really calling about Damian, aren't you?"

She needed to say she'd consigned Damian to

the scrap heap—or pretend that she had. Or least admit they weren't in a real relationship. It was all a mutually-beneficial temporary arrangement, and anything that had happened in the bedroom had been one big mistake… But somehow the words wouldn't come.

"Your father wanted to call, but I said no. 'Serg, *fermati*. Stop.'"

Who was her mother kidding? *Calling* sounded so innocuous. *Yelling*, now that was more like it when it came to her father.

Camilla cleared her throat. "I—how do you say?—reasoned with him. I said, '*I know you are upset*, but Mia will make her decisions and tell us when she's ready.'"

Mia blinked. "Thanks, Mom."

Her mother had always been the one to run interference between her husband and her children, even if she remained a protective parent herself. Over the years, though, Mia had pulled and tugged on familial ties until they had stretched…all the way to New York.

"Did I tell you how your father and I met?" Camilla asked suddenly.

Of course, Mia knew the basic facts, having heard them discussed dozens of times. Her father had been a tourist in Tuscany when he'd first encountered her mother manning the front desk of a hotel. Before he'd checked out, a flame had been lit.

"My family didn't approve of him."

SO RIGHT…WITH MR. WRONG

"You're kidding." This was news to her after thirty years.

"Your father doesn't like to bring it up."

"Of course." Her father had a lot of pride.

"But I had my heart set on Serg."

"Why didn't they approve?"

"They didn't know him, and they were suspicious. Too many Casanovas checked in and out of the *albergo*."

Mia choked back a startled sound. She'd never thought anyone would compare her father to Casanova. Still, she couldn't help being curious. "How did you know that Dad was the one?"

"He was *persistente*." Camilla laughed, her voice full of reminiscence. "I started dating someone else, and your father arranged another stay for himself at the *albergo*."

Damian was nothing if not persistent…

"Anyway, this is about you. I know your father and brothers are worried. You know they don't like the Musils."

"I met them," Mia blurted.

There was silence on the line. "And—"

"Mom, they seemed like any other family in the construction business. Except, you know, it was really up by your bootstraps because Damian's father didn't start his company until he moved to Welsdale. Then he lost his wife and had two young kids to raise."

Mia finished what she was going to say all in one breath. She'd heard enough about Jakob Musil and

JM Construction over the years to know that Damian's father had arrived in Welsdale as a young man—whereas her own father had been born and bred in the area. If any of her relatives could appreciate being a new arrival and settling down in unfamiliar territory, it was her mother.

"Hmm."

Mia could tell her mother was torn between conflicting impulses. Camilla had been thrilled to see her sons married off, and she'd never been shy with questions about whether Mia was dating anyone. But no doubt, she'd never imagined the boyfriend candidate might be Damian Musil.

Wait, there was no candidate. No contender. No contestant.

"I don't know, Mia. Be careful."

Mia could practically picture her mother shaking her head resignedly. "There's nothing to be careful about," she responded lightly. "Damian and I aren't really a couple. We just had…a couple of dates."

There. Vague but accurate.

Her mother sighed, and Mia wondered if that was relief she heard.

"On the other hand, your father and I are heading toward forty-five years—"

"Yup, I know."

"—if we're lucky."

Mia perked up. She was glad for the change of topic, but this sounded *not good.* "*If we're lucky*?"

Her mother sighed. "You know the expression,

no? How do you say? Don't count the eggs before they hatch?"

"Chickens, Mom. Don't count your chickens before they hatch."

"*Sì*, okay. What does it matter? You understand me, no?"

Mia was used to her mother's mashups of Italian and English. "Well, Dad seems to have put his stroke behind him these days," she said carefully, "so there's nothing to worry about, right?"

"Except for his new television career," her mother muttered.

Mia laughed, relaxing. "What? Don't tell me his *Wine Breaks with Serg!* segment has gone to his head?"

"He's giving me advice about my own show."

There'd been a time when her father had seemed threatened by her mother's second act as a local television personality—at the same time that he'd had to step back from the construction company that he'd built. But it had appeared that lately things were going well.

"Next he'll think we're rivals."

"Dad likes to think big. That's how he became a successful business owner. You know, he's competitive."

"Ha! You don't need to tell me."

Honestly, didn't her father's competitive streak also help explain why he'd held tight to his dim view of JM Construction? But on television, her mother was the established player, and her father was the upstart. "Just remind him that he owes his whole show business career to you. Without *Flavors of Italy*, there'd never be a *Wine Breaks with Serg!*"

"You remind him, *cara*," her mother huffed.

"Nice move, Mom. Why don't you let me know when he's ready to talk calmly with me?"

And Mia doubted that her father would appreciate her pointing out that these days he and Jakob Musil had something in common—they were both upstarts.

But he'd welcome any news that she currently had no plans to see Damian again. Now why didn't that make her feel relieved?

Ten

Since the weekend, and especially after the call with her mother, Mia had thrown herself into work.

Still, scenes from the weekend had replayed themselves in her mind, like an auto rewind. They'd pretended to be a couple for the Bensens. And then they'd had a confrontation with her brothers before jumping into an episode of *Meet the Musils!*

Why couldn't she stop thinking about Damian?

Yes, they'd had sex. Yes, it had been good. Yes, it had been spectacular. But now that part was over and never to be repeated…no matter what Damian thought.

Of course, she hadn't heard from him either in over forty-eight hours. And that's exactly how she wanted it, she told herself, unless he was getting in touch about the Bensens and Katie.

She moved bolts of fabric in a corner of her cramped studio, looking for the one that she planned to use for an asymmetrical skirt for her new line. She wanted to expand the range of her business.

The natural light in this ground-level space had never been great, and today was overcast and wet. Maybe she'd walk up the three flights of stairs to her own apartment and work there since she didn't have anyone to supervise today. She was between interns because the school term at the nearby fashion schools was ending.

Her phone buzzed, and she straightened, pushing hair away from her face.

Looking around, she spotted her cell peeking out from underneath a copy of *Brilliance* magazine, which sat atop *Vogue*, *InStyle*, and back issues of some other titles.

Glancing at the screen, she was surprised to discover that the text was from Katie. She sucked in a breath. Alison had insisted on passing along her personal contact info.

The word *interview* jumped out.

Excitement bubbled up.

Then she typed a reply. Sure…

Hitting Send, she blew some lingering stray strands away from her face.

Soon enough, a reply came from Katie.

I'd like to include some words from Damian in the interview. It helps to round it out. I can also reach out to any fashion industry names who'd like to say nice things about you.

Ugh. Mia lowered her shoulders. Damian wasn't really her boyfriend? Instead, she found herself typing again. Sure.

Then she bit her lip. She couldn't even call Gia to talk. Her cousin was abroad—accompanying her husband, Alex, on a brief business trip to Japan. And anyway, there was a good chance Gia would egg her on.

She was about to land a prime spotlight on her company. She was beyond thrilled. But...

Before her bravado failed her, she raised her phone and called.

Thanks to planning for the Ruby Ball, she had Damian's number.

"Hello." The timber of his voice was low, deep, not at all surprised. "Mia."

His voice stole through her like the hit of a shot.

"Katie Bensen wants to interview me," she blurted.

"And that's a bad thing?"

"Yes... No."

"And here I was thinking this was the booty call that I was waiting for."

"Wishful thinking."

"Never stop dreaming."

His irreverence fortified her, and strangely helped overcome her anxiety and misgivings. "I need you—"

"Finally."

"Will you cut it out?"

"Why, when it's so much fun?"

"I need you to be interviewed, too."

"My turn in the limelight," he quipped.

She pasted a tight smile on her face even though he couldn't see it. "*Brilliance* magazine wants to include some words from you because Katie thinks we're—"

"Ah."

"—together," she finished lamely. "Everyone believes you're—"

"A boyfriend," he finished for her.

This was so humiliating. "Thanks partly to you!"

She should have gone with the idea of hiring a model or escort to accompany her to the Ruby Ball. Now Katie had recommended making Damian a part of the magazine piece…and she'd agreed, jumping at a chance that was too good to pass up.

And, really, what else could she have said? No doubt the readers of *Brilliance* would savor every word about Damian… *If only they knew.* Their coupledom was a stunt. But if she was lucky, maybe a few of those single readers would contact him. The thought left a sour taste.

"All right, I have a suggestion."

Mia stilled.

"You conduct the interview at my offices."

"That's it?" She dropped her shoulders. The truth was, she hadn't relished the possibility of an interview in her cramped studio—one where she and an intern often had to sidestep each other.

"If you're doing the interview here, it'll lend credibility to our—"

"Coupledom?"

"Connection."

"Like the One Republic song?"

"You're a fan?"

"I have wide musical tastes. I was the designated DJ at slumber parties." When she hadn't been sneaking backstage at rock concerts...

Damian's rich laugh felt like a warm embrace. Then he started humming "All I Ever Need Is You."

His voice spread through her...heating, warming, kindling her senses. He had her off-balance, and thinking back to their weekend together, though she would never admit it. "You're going to make this ask as hard as possible, aren't you?"

Damian's voice trailed off. "Drop me a text with the details, and I'll arrange an empty office space to conduct the interview."

"Great." She paused a beat. "Thanks."

"No problem. And since we're exchanging favors—"

"Exchanging?" Why did that word sound foreboding?

"I've got a charity dinner to attend at the end of next week. A lot of the East Coast tech crowd will be there. The extra ticket is yours."

Wait—what? It sounded a lot like...a date. "We're not a couple. We agreed."

"Did we?"

"You know we did. Or I said it, and you didn't disagree. So it was a meeting of the minds."

She pulled her thoughts away from the other ways they'd made a connection last weekend…

"Maybe I'm clueless."

"Oh, puh-leeze."

He gave a low laugh. "You don't believe me? It was just me, Dad and Valentin over at the Musil shack."

She snapped her mouth shut—chagrined. *Of course.* He'd lost his mother, and hadn't she spotted his remembrance necklace this weekend? But he couldn't be that clueless about women…could he?

She'd grown up with three older brothers who were all smooth guys, able to charm their way through innumerable girlfriends. Of course, her brothers had all been in the public eye and magnets for the opposite gender. Cole and Jordan had played for the NHL, and Rick had spent time as a stuntman with name-brand actresses on the big screen.

"On the other hand, you were holed up in the Serenghetti castle."

"Hardly."

He cut off a laugh. "I'm supposed to say I agree, right?"

"See, you are a quick study."

"What if I claimed I've learned a lot from you?"

She shivered with awareness even as she felt flustered by the flattery. For a guy who hadn't grown up around women, he was doing just *fine*. So instead of answering him directly, she said, "Fine, if that's what it takes to make this interview happen, get back to me with the details about the dinner."

"Great."

Just what she thought he might say. Sweet heaven...

Mia sat across from Katie in one of the empty glass-walled conference rooms at CyberSilver Technologies. They were taking a break from the interview so Katie could review her notes. The room was spare, as befitted a cutting-edge tech company, but plenty of light filtered in from the pre-war building's generous windows overlooking Fifth Avenue from twenty-three stories above.

Damian's employees walked by outside. They were dressed casually and seemed very laid-back, like they weren't at work. She could see them through the glass walls, but they couldn't hear her.

Fortunately. If they wondered what she and *Katie* were doing in their offices, no one said anything.

They could read all about it in *Brilliance*. And then she'd have some quick footwork and explaining to do with her family. She'd left her mother with the impression there was nothing to be concerned about beyond a few dates that had fizzled...

She'd have to claim that she and Damian had delayed their conscious uncoupling. She almost winced at the increasing tangle that she had to extricate herself from...

Mia shifted on her stool. It was hard to relax when this interview was so fraught with potential pitfalls.

So far, she'd been able to toss out some good details about her business in response to Katie's questions. Her brand was affordable, environmentally conscious, and easy to wear. She'd hit all the keywords, sprinkling her answers with the bold terms in her business plan. All her best designs were displayed on some mannequins in the room. A photographer and assistant from *Brilliance* were busy photographing them. She'd also already emailed some pictures to the magazine.

Katie flipped a page in her notepad and looked up. "Ready to resume the interview?"

"Sure!" Had she sounded peppy enough?

"So tell me how you and Damian met," Katie gushed.

Huh? The questioning had suddenly taken a dangerous turn, and Mia straightened. "We grew up in the same town in Massachusetts, so, uh, of course we knew of each other."

"But there wasn't a spark of attraction back then?"

"Well, no." *Liar, liar.*

"We don't see you two together often. He doesn't show up on your social media."

"We wanted to keep our relationship private until now." *Yeah, right.* They'd done a crummy job keeping their nonrelationship under wraps. The people whom she wanted most of all to keep in the dark—her family—had found out anyway.

"Isn't social media how you got your start in fashion?" Katie asked, changing her tactics.

Mia nodded. *Phew.* At least they were off the topic of Damian. "I started out as an influencer back in high school and college. Then I kept building a following." She laughed. "I spent too much time on filming videos and not so much on chemistry."

Katie grinned. "Me, too. Well, not so much making my own stuff, but posting what I liked about other designs. I guess my father was disappointed. I didn't show much interest in the family company."

Mia found herself warming to Katie Bensen even apart from their work-related connection. "Hey, it's okay." She shrugged. "I wasn't much into construction, which was my family's business. The way I see it, I liked to create stuff but with different materials."

"So how do you stay fresh? With designs, I mean?"

"I take inspiration where I find it. It could be the color of a sunset." Or the look and feel of a thunderstorm on a night when you were trying not to be aware of temptation sleeping a few feet away.

At the sound of the door opening, they both turned. Damian sauntered in, looking every inch the rich tech startup owner, dressed down in jeans and an open-collar shirt. Since the interview was being conducted at CyberSilver, everyone had agreed that Damian would stop by in person for some questions from Katie.

There was an air of authority about Damian here in his corporate headquarters that was downplayed when he was socializing outside work. With her fashion eye, though, Mia could tell his shoes were expensive and his shirt was impeccably tailored—

which helped advertise the lithe, muscular physique that she was all too well acquainted with.

Her heartbeat ticked up a notch.

She'd dressed carefully for this interview—striving for professional but edgy to match her brand. She'd finally settled on a black-and-white jumpsuit. The black trousers were attached to a white bodice with a sweetheart neckline and short puff sleeves. The bottom was conservative, but the top looked as if it could have been cut off a bridal dress. The construction was clever; it looked like two pieces when it was actually one, since jumpsuits had started as her signature item and her market niche...

She'd thought she'd hit the right note sartorially. But she hadn't anticipated Damian's look of appreciation—as if he was drinking her in.

He quickly replaced it with a bland expression and came toward her with a slight smile.

She shifted again on her seat and wished that she'd thought of nudging the empty stool next to her farther away. So she could breathe, think, focus.

Damian stopped next to her and leaned down. She widened her eyes.

He brushed her lips with his. "Hi, babe."

She sucked in a breath, and he gave her a slightly crooked smile.

Babe...? And what was he up to with the public display of affection?

When he sat next to her, she crossed her legs.

"I'm so glad you could join us," Katie bubbled.

"And thanks for the use of your office. Mia suggested we'd be more comfortable here."

Mia avoided Damian's laughing eyes.

"No problem," he responded easily. "Anything to help."

Katie looked between them. "How long have you two been dating, if I can ask? I couldn't find anything about you before the Ruby Ball."

Mia knew she had to jump in. "Not long—"

"But I've been watching Mia forever."

Katie perked up. "Waiting for your chance?"

Along with Katie, Mia turned to look at Damian.

"Well, Mia was dating my former employee. You may have heard of him, Carl Eshoo."

Katie leaned forward. "Ooh, a love triangle."

"Not quite," Mia said hurriedly.

What was this? A fashion profile or a gossip piece?

Katie looked down at the pad in her hand. "My research showed he and Mia were an item—" she glanced at Mia apologetically "—but Carl recently got married."

So Katie had done her homework.

"His loss, my gain."

Wow, Damian was laying it on thick.

"But wait," Katie persisted, glancing from Mia to Damian and back, "if you've known each other for a long time, why did things never, uh, happen between you?"

Crap. "We were like two ships passing in the night—"

"And our families didn't like each other."

Mia resisted the urge to kick him. If she swung her crossed leg, could she make it look like an accident if it connected with his shin?

Katie, though, leaned back with delight. "Oh, so romantic. Like Romeo and Juliet."

Mia moved her elbow in position to give Damian a poke. He was inches away…but she had no room for error with a stealth maneuver.

"And it's so cute the way you finish each other's sentences."

Mia gave the semblance of a smile. "Isn't it just?"

This was playing out to her advantage in at least one way, she belatedly realized. The story now wasn't that she'd been dumped by a guy who'd raced to the altar with someone else. Instead, she'd moved on with the boss—who'd had the hots for her all along. While her family would have a conniption, the *Brilliance* readers would love it.

But what was Damian up to? It was one thing to tease her in bed about how he'd always been attracted to her. It was another to lay it on thick for a reporter…

Katie leaned in. "So your families are what kept you apart."

"Well, I can't speak for Mia," Damian demurred, "but I was crushing on her."

Both Katie and Damian turned to look at her, and Mia wet her lips.

"I, uh, was oblivious?" She tacked on a small laugh.

Damian lifted the side of his mouth. "Babe, you know I'm usually subtle—"

As a sledgehammer.

"—but you definitely had the hots for me."

She blinked at him—hard.

Katie, though, seemed to be eating up every juicy, duplicitous morsel.

Mia smiled brightly at the younger woman. "Well, there you have it. Damian is subtle…and I'm not."

Katie laughed. "Sort of like the Mia Serenghetti brand?"

As Mia widened her eyes, Damian nodded and folded his arms. "Bold, brave and badass."

Eleven

"I've instructed my lawyers to get everything in order for the closing date that we agreed to," Larry Bensen said, sounding pleasant and relaxed over the phone.

Damian sank back against his office chair. "Great. I'm looking forward to it. How does it feel now that things are nearly settled?"

Larry chuckled. "Like a weight has almost lifted from my shoulders."

"The company will be in good hands, Larry."

"I'm counting on it."

"I'm from Welsdale. It's important to me to help preserve the town and to keep connected to it." This was as personal as he'd ever gotten in a business deal.

"I figured as much."

They talked some more about the closing, and when the call ended, Damian rubbed the back of his neck.

The business with Larry was as good as a done deal. All they needed was for the lawyers to finish the drafting of purchase documents. Because Larry had been ready to sell and had been looking for a buyer, he'd already had his house in order. With any luck, now the deal would close on time and without a hitch.

Soon, very soon, Damian would be the new owner of a local Welsdale television station. The native son done good and come home. The name Musil would be associated with a whole new venture and industry. Short of sticking his name on a park, street or impressive downtown building—but that might come in time—he'd gone a long way toward bolstering the family name. On top of it, he'd be investing in his hometown, which had helped mold him into who he was.

Damian thought back to Mia, because that's where his mind often went these days.

The interview with Katie had gone great. Sure, he'd laid it on a little thick—he could see the sparks in Mia's eyes when he'd called her *babe*—but he hadn't lied, either.

Because this was no longer solely about a business deal with Larry Bensen—if it ever was. Somewhere along the way, Damian acknowledged, his motives had morphed.

This was about the Serenghettis and Musils, and

the fact that he and Mia had been dancing around each other for years because they'd gotten tangled up in simmering family rivalries.

Damian steepled his fingers, and then turned his chair to look out the windows behind his office desk. And now, damn it, that rivalry had raised its head again, threatening to upend things. Because JM Construction and Serenghetti Construction were vying to purchase the same company.

No doubt Mia's family was unhappy about her seeing him. He knew Mia was a rebel who'd buck any heavy-handed demand they made, but then again, he hadn't gotten to the top of the corporate world by letting the chips fall where they may. He needed a counterbalance.

Swinging around again, he tightened his hands on the chair rests. *Alex McDonough*.

The thought had first occurred to him before the call with Larry.

Alex was the husband of Mia's cousin, Gia Serenghetti. He'd crossed paths with him at tech gatherings over the years and respected him. More importantly, he knew Mia was close to her cousin— he'd seen them with their heads together at more than one New York party over the years. And he'd bought a whole table at this charity dinner and still had seats to fill…

He clicked on his computer mouse and opened a window to start an email to Alex. He quickly typed a few lines and then clicked to send. Then he leaned back, satisfied. *Almost*.

When he got his father on the phone, they exchanged pleasantries. Now that Jakob Musil was older, he stuck closer to JM Construction's management offices and delegated, so it didn't completely surprise Damian that he was able to get his father on a call on the first attempt.

"So," he said after they'd been on the phone a few minutes, "how are things going with the purchase of Tevil Construction?"

"They're no longer for sale."

Damian let silence reign for a moment. "So they've decided to go with the Serenghettis' offer?"

"I didn't say that," Jakob responded gruffly. "They've taken themselves off the market. They're no longer for sale."

Damian blew out a breath. "Well, that takes care of that problem."

"Maybe for you, but not for me. JM Construction needs to grow."

Damian zeroed in on the first part of his father's statement. "Maybe for me? You're suggesting—"

"If I had won the bid for Tevil Construction, it would have made complications for you with Mia Serenghetti."

True, but lately, his concerns were more nuanced. "I guess there's a silver lining."

"And you're wise these days, too."

Damian ignored the note of sarcasm. "Dad, you're sixty-two. Maybe it's time to start taking it easy instead of trying to expand the business."

"What?"

"Serg Serenghetti is already retired."

"He's older than I am. And he had a stroke." Jakob made a grumbling sound. "Besides, Serg has a son to run the company now."

"You've got Valentin."

"He just came aboard. How do you say? Reluctantly."

Damian knew his brother had kicked around bars in Welsdale, Springfield and beyond, playing gigs with his band and generally doing a good impression of being a footloose rocker. Still. "Listen, Dad, maybe Tevil is a headache that you're better off without."

Damian could practically hear his father's eyebrows lower over the phone.

"You should be getting ready to enjoy your golden years." Winding things down. *Like Larry Bensen.*

"So you jump ship, but now you want to advise me on how to steer?"

"Anyway, are you sure buying this company wasn't just about the satisfaction of outflanking the Serenghettis?"

Jakob spluttered. "Who put that foolish idea in your mind? Mia?"

"No, I came up with the dumb thought all by myself."

His father guffawed.

"I've got some good news for you." This should buoy his father and take his mind off Tevil. "I'm buying the local television station."

"What? Which?"

"WBEN-TV."

"I don't watch much television. Too busy with work."

Precisely my point earlier. There was no doubt he'd gotten his work ethic from his father.

"So you'll be back in Welsdale now with this company."

Damian found himself nodding against the phone. "Maybe not in the way you expected, but I'll be local."

"I always knew you'd come back." There was a bark of laughter. "Ah."

Damian smiled.

"The Musils are going into the television business."

"I guess they are, Dad."

"Did you open the box that I gave you?" Jakob asked, switching gears.

"Yes." It was no longer so painful to think of his mother. In fact, the memories brought fondness as much as sadness these days.

"Your mother wanted you to have them when you got married—"

What?

"—or you and Valentin reached thirty. You know which happened first."

Yup. He'd been working nonstop for years—until recently. Sure, he and Mia had started as a pretend couple for business reasons, but she'd soon become his focus.

His mother would have liked Mia.

Damian sighed and then answered his father. "I'm not sad when I think of Mom now. Maybe that's why I'm coming back. And to make her proud."

"*I'm* proud of you."

"I couldn't have done it without you, Dad."

Damian realized this was as close as he and his father had come—since he'd moved away from Welsdale—to acknowledging how much they were still connected.

"I'm glad to hear it," Jakob said gruffly.

"You've got to save me," Mia announced.

Then she knocked back some wine that she'd brought with her before her gaze connected with Gia's in the powder room mirror.

"Mmm," her cousin commented as she reapplied lipstick.

Beyond the hushed and upholstered confines of the anteroom to the ladies' restroom, hundreds of people dined at tables whose price per plate would certainly make her head spin, Mia thought. Gotham Hall was one of the city's premier event spaces—a nine-thousand-square-foot ballroom under a stained-glass dome. Its imposing neoclassical facade was a Broadway landmark.

Not that she knew the precise price tag of being here tonight. Damian had arranged everything. In fact, she'd been surprised to discover, when she'd arrived, that Gia and Alex were here, too, and seated at the same table. *She'd* only agreed to show up in a deal with the devil.

Or so she tried to convince herself. The words rang hollow to her own ears. But the more she tried to extricate herself from her ties to Damian, the more entangled she seemed to become. He was seductive and enticing.

She touched the fine filigree diamond necklace at her throat—one that came with matching earrings. *Another loan from the jewelers,* Damian had said. They had shown up at her door by courier after Damian had texted her to ask what color she'd be wearing tonight. She'd assumed he'd asked so that he could coordinate his own attire—not for the sake of picking out precious gemstones for her.

Of course, since she'd gotten to know him better, she'd come to respect and...appreciate him. He wasn't a bad guy just because of his last name— if she'd ever believed that to be the case. He'd defended her to her family, had her back with Carl and even been a pretend boyfriend during her interview with Katie.

But anything more was too fraught with pitfalls...too everything, for that matter. They could remain acquainted—friends even. She stiffened at the thought of Damian dating another woman, and then shrugged off the feeling.

Gia deposited her makeup in her handbag. "I think things are going well."

"Are you kidding?" Mia responded. "The evening has just begun, and Damian and I are practically striking sparks off each other."

Gia tossed her a sidelong look. "You know, I was

surprised when Alex told me that Damian had offered us seats at his table for this event, especially since I'm a Serenghetti cousin and know all about the animosity between your family and his."

Mia turned wide eyes on her cousin. "He offered you seats?"

Gia smirked. "You didn't think it was a coincidence that Alex and I are here tonight, did you? No, we didn't buy seats ourselves. But why didn't you mention that *you* would be here?"

"Why didn't you?" Mia flushed. "Anyway, you were out of the country traveling. You were hard to get a hold of."

"And yet Damian managed to get off an email invite to Alex while we were in Japan."

Guilty. She'd been keeping mum about her relationship with Damian. It wasn't that she didn't trust Gia. It was that talking about it would lead to questions that she wasn't prepared to answer. She wasn't even sure if she had all the answers.

"Then I realized that Alex and I may have been invited precisely because I'm a Serenghetti, not despite it."

Mia blinked. "What do you mean?"

Her cousin gave her a disbelieving look. "Mia, the guy seems hooked on you. But he also knows your immediate family is suspicious of him. Obviously, Alex and I are here to help smooth things. It might make you more comfortable, and Damian could try to win over some of your other relatives."

Mia was floored. She'd just assumed earlier that

since this was a big event for the tech industry, Alex had decided to show up and had brought Gia. Had Damian really gone to so much trouble for her...?

Her cousin tossed her another sidelong look. "I see you took my advice that Damian might be worth more than one date."

"Whose side are you on?"

"Yours of course."

"You could have fooled me," Mia muttered under her breath.

"I never really liked Carl."

"Now you tell me?" Mia peered at herself critically in the mirror. "Next to Damian, he's a domesticated kitten."

"Exactly. Carl was too tame for you."

"So he got hitched to someone else to get away from the wild cat?"

Gia smiled. "Is that what Damian thinks of you?"

Mia flushed. "Who? Damian the tamer?"

Gia laughed. "He's got an appropriate name. Not boring."

Like Carl. Mia heard her cousin's unspoken words.

"Maybe he's got the right temperament for the boardroom," she huffed. "But he's got another think coming if he aims to tame a Serenghetti."

"From the way he was looking at you during dinner," Gia murmured, "that's not what he has in mind. Eat you up is more like it."

Mia turned to face Gia. "Right, and this has to stop."

"Why?"

"He's a Musil." *And so many other reasons.* He unsettled her. He got under her skin.

"So you're not supposed to trust him but you want to, um, make it with him?"

She'd already done the deed with him—and it had been spectacular. And from all appearances, he wanted to be invited back for more. "He's…unpredictable."

She adjusted the shoulder strap of her dress.

"I think," Gia said, gazing at Mia's gown, "in this case you were done in by your own sartorial skills. Damian's reaction is very predictable…"

Mia bunched the skirt of her dress in one hand. "What? This?" *This old thing?* "I designed it for my senior project at Parsons years ago."

She had *not* gone to any great lengths to please Damian tonight.

"How can I forget?" her cousin responded lightly. "But cleavage never goes out of style."

Okay, so the gown was daring—but that had been the point when she'd been trying to earn a top grade at Parsons. She'd been a twenty-two-year-old who'd been starry-eyed at the end of a four-year college stint in New York City.

The neckline of the gown plunged between her breasts in the front and even lower in the back. The bodice was a deep blue velvet and the skirt a waterfall of tulle in an ombre pattern that ended in the palest of aqua at her feet. She'd had to use fashion tape to keep everything in place because she'd gotten curvier in the years since she'd graduated.

"You look like a mermaid emerging from the waves."

"Thanks for remembering my thesis show," Mia remarked dryly. "But did you have to mention it to Damian, too?"

Gia gave an impish smile. "Just making conversation. He seemed to...admire the handiwork."

Mia rolled her eyes. "I'm supposed to be the one who makes waves."

Gia laughed. "What can I say? Marriage agrees with me. I've started living outside the boxes of the comic strip that I draw. In fact, you should try it."

Mia widened her eyes. "What? Marriage?"

Gia turned to leave. "No, sex with a guy who gets hot under the collar merely looking at you."

Mia clamped her mouth shut. If only her cousin knew. Damian didn't just get hot under the collar, he got her hot...all over. Where was water to douse the flames when she needed it?

When she and Gia eventually got back to their table, Damian threw her simmering look, and Mia took another gulp of her wine.

Her cousin tossed her an amused little smile from across the table, and Mia responded with a small frown.

Glancing around, Mia spotted Carl and his wife chatting with other guests a few tables away. She nearly groaned aloud. *Great.* As if this evening could get any more awkward.

Carl was part of the tech world, too, and he and Damian likely still moved in overlapping circles…

Pasting a smile on her face, she leaned toward Damian. Obligingly, he tilted in her direction, giving her his ear. His closeness made her breasts tingle.

"I didn't know Carl was going to be here," she murmured.

Raising his gaze, he gave her quizzical look. "Neither did I. Problem?"

Of course not.

Damian glanced past her. "Here they come."

Next thing she knew, Damian was draping an arm along the back of her chair, his fingers grazing her exposed spine in a passing caress.

When Carl hailed them, Damian turned and stood, and Mia reluctantly followed, depositing her napkin beside her plate. Damian slipped his arm around her in a signal of…support…affection?

Catching the interested expression on Gia's face, Mia could tell her cousin was savoring the show.

Drat.

Damian and Carl shook hands.

For the first time, Mia got a good look at Carl's wife. The woman she'd built up to be a bit of a femme fatale was actually…a bespectacled and feminine version of Carl. Curly dark hair framed her face in a style that was too wild to be a true pixie cut, and big brown eyes peeked at her from behind large frames.

It seemed, Mia thought bemusedly, she'd been

dumped for someone who seemed to be Carl's complete counterpart.

"Laura, this is Mia Serenghetti," Carl said, looking a bit sheepish. "Ah…"

Laura jumped into the gap, grasping Mia's outstretched hand in both of hers and leaning in with an earnest smile. "It's such a pleasure to meet you."

Mia couldn't detect any smugness, just sincere interest. Laura hadn't gone with the tried-and-true *I've heard so much about you*, which would have been awkward under the circumstances.

"It's nice to meet you, too," Mia murmured.

"We were making the rounds of, ah, the tables," Carl put in, "and thought we'd, ah, say hello."

"I'm such a fan of your work," Laura said, still grasping her hand.

"You are?" Mia couldn't keep the shocked surprise from her voice.

Laura nodded, finally dropping her hand. "Yes. I was at your fashion show two years ago with friends. I own a jumpsuit from the collection that you showed."

"Oh!" Bemusement turned to feeling flattered. If the timeline was right, Laura had known of her even before she'd met Carl.

"When Carl mentioned that he'd once dated you, I couldn't believe it." Laura's eyes sparkled behind her glasses.

Judging from the way Carl blanched, it seemed he hadn't gone into too many details with Laura about the precise timeline of his breakup.

Mia knew she had to play along; forgiveness was the best policy. "You should come by my studio for another jumpsuit." She winked. "Consider it a wedding gift."

Carl looked relieved, while Damian tossed her an amused look.

"I couldn't," Laura protested. "I know a boutique in Midtown that carries your designs—"

Mia waved a hand. "I'll be sending out next season's styles soon. I'll give you a peek."

Laura nodded. "Oh, right. You mentioned it in *Brilliance* magazine."

Mia blinked. "You read it?"

The issue with her interview wasn't supposed to be out until—

"They posted a teaser on their website."

Mia stilled. She needed to get her cell phone.

Carl and Damian made some small talk for a few more minutes.

Then Carl touched Laura's arm. "Well, it was great to run into you guys. We're going to keep circulating."

Carl and Damian shook hands before the other couple moved off.

Mia caught Gia's expression as she sat back down. Her cousin looked as if she could barely contain her curiosity.

"I guess that's what they call *conscious uncoupling*?" Damian murmured, retaking his seat.

"Who, me and Carl…?" Ironically, that's what she'd vowed she and Damian would do—first after the Ruby Ball, and then after Katie's interview. Except here they were.

Mia pulled up *Brilliance*'s web site on her phone and, after a quick scan of links, found the mention of her interview.

"Who else?" Damian replied dryly. "Well done, by the way. A lot harder to hold a grudge when you meet the enemy like that, isn't it?"

"Yup." She held up her phone. "And speaking of enemies, thanks to Katie's interview, everyone thinks the Serenghettis and Musils are lovers, not fighters."

Twelve

"So this is how the rich live."

"No, this is how I live," Damian corrected.

Mia placed her evening bag on the entry table and swiveled to face Damian.

She shivered. His penthouse duplex was in a new luxury tower. The condo was cool, muted and dim. The lights of the city twinkled outside sprawling windows.

"Cold?"

Must his voice be so sexy? "No, I'm fine."

While Damian consulted the apps on his cell phone, Mia took a moment to gather herself.

All during their chauffeured car ride back from the charity event, she'd mulled what she wanted to say, examined her feelings and tried to think things through. It was why she'd suggested going to his place. If Damian had been surprised—pleased?—he hadn't questioned her decision. The truth was, at his place, she was in control of when to end things and leave.

Mia heard the air conditioner in the condo picking up. Then velvet curtains automatically drew closed in the living room adjacent to the entry foyer. He was certainly high tech—but then what else should she have expected?

She pivoted. "Does the fireplace magically turn on? And where's the faint music? The lights are already dim, though."

He raised an eyebrow at her, amused...and a touch sheepish? "Drink?"

"No, thank you."

He paused.

She cleared her throat. Because she knew what she was here to do. She'd already ignored one *how's it going?* text from Gia.

Tilting her head forward to expose her nape, she removed the diamond necklace and then the earrings. Then she held them out to him. *She'd loved them.* Just as she had with the pieces for the Ruby Ball. "Thank you for another loan."

His lips twitched in wry amusement, but he took the jewelry—their fingers brushing—and pocketed them as if they were no more than plastic prizes dispensed by a toy vending machine.

"I wanted to talk."

"Problem?" Damian asked levelly.

She drew in a deep breath. "Thanks for giving me a graceful but public way tonight to put Carl in the rearview mirror. I know news of our crossing paths with the Eshoos will eventually filter out to people who know us."

He gave an imperceptible nod.

"And thanks for helping me open doors with Katie, and…having my back with my family when we were up in Welsdale."

"That's three thank-yous in a row. So why do I think a kiss-off is coming?" he teased, his voice nevertheless holding a note of gravity.

There wouldn't be any kissing. That was the point.

"Let me guess—you're troubled because you realized that you built up the breakup with Carl to more than it was."

She shook her head—more vehemently than she'd meant to, so locks of hair tumbled around her shoulders. "No, I realized that the reason it bothered me so much was that *you* were involved."

Damian stilled and then his eyes gleamed. "Ah."

"Ah? That's it?"

"I'm hesitating in case I say the wrong thing."

"When have you ever let that stop you?"

He cut off a laugh. "I'm learning." Then he sobered and came closer, so she could still feel the energy coming off him, but didn't touch her. "And now? Does it still bother you?"

Her shoulders sagged and she blew a breath. "Carl's not the enemy…and neither are you even though I lumped you in with your family for a long time." She shrugged. "So of course when you were advising and helping Carl, I was suspicious."

"If I'm not the enemy, then what am I?" he asked softly.

Friend...lover. She raised her hands as if to hold him off, even though he hadn't taken another step. "This has gotten complicated—"

"Complicated is good," he joked.

"How can you say that?"

He lightly clasped her wrist and drew her even closer.

"Bold, brave and badass, really?" she argued faintly.

Damian smiled. "Those were my words, yes."

"It's also the headline of Katie's story, which is already live or at least teased on the *Brilliance* web site."

"Great."

"You have a starring role."

He studied her mouth. "Consider me flattered."

The back of her neck tingled with an awareness that soon seeped into other parts of her...

"You laid it on thick with Katie."

"That's assuming I didn't mean what I said."

"And that endearment—"

Damian laced his fingers with hers. *"Babe."*

What was she going to do with a man who could disarm her so easily? "You're—"

"Irresistible, irrepressible...irreplaceable?"

"It's so cute the way that we finish each other's

sentences…" She made a halfhearted attempt at scoffing about Katie's comment.

He drew her into his arms. "No…it's so great the way that we make each other feel."

"Feel…is that what we do?"

"And kiss," he muttered. "Don't forget that."

He searched her gaze, and reading her eyes, bent his head.

She swallowed hard, moments before his lips settled on hers, and then twisted her hands in his lapels.

Damian made a sound at the back of his throat, and she sighed. There was a desperate, feverish quality to their kiss, as if hours at a stuffy industry dinner, politely listening to speaker after speaker, had fueled their suppressed need.

When they finally broke apart, Damian nuzzled the hair at her temple. Even in heels, she was three or four inches shorter.

"I'll make you a deal," he said huskily.

"Another one?"

He smiled against her hair. "You can invent a name for me, too. What do you want to call me?"

Tamer. "Insufferable?"

"Try harder, it doesn't roll off the tongue."

She was dimly aware that his hands were roaming, caressing her bare back as if looking for a zipper. *Or a key to her heart.*

He feathered kisses along the side of her face and down her neck. "Well?"

"I'm still thinking." She tilted her neck to accommodate him, letting her hair fall back.

"Ah, Mia."

Finally, when his hands came to rest on her shoulders, she had mercy on him. "Everything is held in place with fashion tape."

He muttered an expletive. "Tape doesn't belong on skin."

"It's an industry trick to prevent wardrobe malfunctions."

He looked at her with hooded eyes. "Hey, I like clothing...with glitches."

A breathless laugh escaped her. "You were right. I came here to give you the kiss-off..."

He raised his brows above smoky eyes. "Well, there'll be kissing and some things are coming off."

Holding his gaze, she placed her hands over his on her shoulders, and together they pulled apart her bodice.

He groaned. "Babe, you're bold, brave and badass."

Then he bent and trailed his lips down her cleavage, and her head fell back.

When Damian pulled her bodice all the way off so that the shoulder straps landed on her wrists, he inhaled sharply. The pads of his thumbs grazed her nipples, and then he settled his mouth over one breast.

She rested her forearms on his shoulders, losing herself in a fog of need.

When he finally straightened, he gave her a hard kiss, letting her feel his hunger.

Her fingers began to work at the buttons on his

white shirt, and he shrugged out of his tuxedo jacket, letting it fall to the floor.

"I don't want to ruin the work of art that you're wearing," he murmured. "Someone will want to display your senior project in an exhibition someday."

"I can't believe Gia told you."

Damian nodded. "She noticed how I couldn't take my eyes off you in that dress."

"And that you wanted to get me out of it," Mia added, and then gave him an openmouthed kiss.

He lifted her off her feet and strode deeper into the dark recesses of the penthouse.

Moments later, Mia lifted her head and realized they were in Damian's oversized bedroom. White upholstery and bedding contrasted with dark-paneled wood. The lights of the city twinkled behind pale window blinds.

Slowly he lowered her so that her feet touched the floor again, letting her feel every inch of him on the slow slide to the ground.

He wanted her. That much was obvious.

Holding his gaze, she lowered the tiny hidden zipper at the side of her waist, and the whole dress fell in a heap at her feet, leaving her standing in panties and high-heeled sandals.

She forced herself to hold still under his hot gaze and lifted her chin a notch.

"You're beautiful," he said hoarsely.

"Now that's a b-word that you didn't use," she teased. "How did you leave out *beautiful* during the interview?"

Damian groaned self-deprecatingly, and then ran his fingers up and down her arms, before slipping them under the fabric of her panties and following the hourglass figure created by her waist. "Believe me, by the time we're done, you're going to hear a lot more from me."

She stroked the length of his erection. "Because you're *bothered*?"

He pulled his shirt out of his waistband. "How can you tell?"

She wet her lips, her mouth suddenly dry, and swallowed.

He tossed his shirt aside. "Step out of those blue waves pooling at your feet...*beautiful*."

She did, kicking off one sandal and then the other, and then he swung her up and deposited her on the bed.

"You need to stop carrying me."

"See, that's where we disagree. I haven't done it enough."

When he started to strip, she sat up straighter and then stood. "Let me."

She undid his belt and then he shucked his pants and briefs, stepping out of his shoes and pulling off his socks with them.

"Let me do this," she said throatily, stroking his rigid length.

His eyes flared and then closed on a hiss. "Ah, Mia."

She bent and her mouth closed around him.

She worked his length, and Damian made some

guttural sounds. She savored the experience of making *him* weak.

Finally, he hauled her up, but when he would have tossed her on the bed again, she instead pushed him to a sitting position on the edge and straddled him.

Their mouths tangled, and the momentum sent him back against the bed.

"I've got to be inside you," he said on a half laugh with an edge of desperation.

She'd never heard Damian desperate before. *Desperate for her.* He was always so cool and in control—or seemed to be.

"I'm on the pill," she whispered against his mouth. "And I have a clean bill of health."

"Yeah, clean bill, too," he said thickly.

She guided him inside her, and they both sighed. She moved then, and he directed her with his hands on her hips, setting a rhythm that they both enjoyed.

Distantly from the other room, her cell phone buzzed, and she ignored it. The last thing she needed was for reality to intrude. This was about her and Damian…and now. A time and place where they didn't have last names, histories, animosities…

"Ignore it," he gritted, having the same idea.

"Yes," she whispered against his mouth.

He moved again, rocking against her, setting off tiny spasms of sensation that grew in ferocity as they fanned out through every inch of her body.

She called his name with her release, and with a final thrust, Damian came inside her, losing himself. They held each other while waves of emotion and sensation washed over them.

In his mind, the past couple of weeks had been a vacation.

Still, freshly showered, Damian threw on some clothes at Mia's place because he knew he'd have to get to the office soon.

He and Mia had fallen into a pattern of getting together without any discussion of the heavy issues that might still hang between them—or more particularly, between their families. Instead they'd lived in the moment...casually eating out, going for a bike ride near the High Line, or most recently, a concert at Madison Square Garden, where they'd sat by themselves in the CyberSilver box. Usually they'd end up at his place or hers, where they hadn't been able to keep their hands off each other.

They'd talked business occasionally, and he'd given her advice—one entrepreneur to another. He'd also put her in touch with his contacts—someone to review company finances, another to consult on marketing.

He looked around the bedroom of the walkup apartment now and spotted his wallet where he'd tossed it on a dresser last night. With a small smile, he retrieved it from where it peeked out from under Mia's bra.

Her bedroom was a small space at the back of an already-small apartment. The bed was covered with fluffy white counterpane that pooled on the floor like an oversized wedding dress. It was offset by exposed gray brick walls, a polished gray wood floor, and some dark furniture. Exactly what he would have expected from Mia: feminine but edgy.

Except he'd now breached the inner sanctum—so the sheets were mussed, thanks to their night together. Afterward, she'd curled up against him, their hearts beating in counterpoint as they'd drifted off to sleep.

Mia bounced into the room, her face lit up with excitement. "Good news. I got an email from a department store buyer. She saw Katie's article and wants to place a big order." She gave him an endearingly tentative smile. "I'm starting out in a few of their locations, so we'll see how things go."

He slipped his arms around her. "Congratulations. The start of something big."

She placed her hands on his chest. "I've got to get in touch with the factory today. There's no time to lose."

He gave her a quick kiss. "You'll be great. I have total faith in you." Then he smiled wolfishly. "But speaking of good news and the start of something."

Playfully, she pulled out of his arms and wagged a finger at him. "We've both got work to do."

He sighed good-naturedly. "Tonight then. I'll pick you up."

Twenty minutes later, she walked him downstairs so he could hail a cab to work, and she could unlock the street entrance to her ground-floor studio and start her day.

At the sidewalk, she clung to him for another kiss and then turned away toward her workspace.

Damian stepped into the street to flag a cab, but within moments, he heard someone call Mia's name.

A male someone.

He turned around and caught Mia's surprised look from where she had swiveled away from her front door.

"Sam."

Crap. So there really was a Sam. And he was back home. *Great timing.*

Damian sized up the other man, who—grinning from ear to ear—made his way toward Mia. Damian dropped his arm and curled his hand by his side. No way in hell was he missing this action.

Mia gave Sam a tight smile. "You're back. From Japan."

Yeah, this was awkward. Damian would give her that. Unfortunately only two out of three of them knew it. Sam kept steaming forward toward Mia like a train that could not be derailed.

"Yup, here I am." He threw his arms out expansively.

Damian's gaze connected with Mia's. *Wow, you sure can pick them.*

She frowned at him, and then directed a pleasant if uncomfortable look at Sam. "This is—"

"Yeah, I know." Sam grinned. "Surprise." He gestured to the door behind Mia. "I took a detour from my regular route to the office and stopped in the coffee shop across the street for a quick bagel since you weren't at work yet." Sam jerked his head to indicate the general direction that he'd come from, completely missing Damian.

Damian was hit by a mixture of skepticism and jealousy. She was going to show up at the Ruby Ball with this guy? *He* was the competition? Damian could see the passing resemblance between him and Sam in height and build—and especially in dim lighting and with a mask on at a costume party—but he was hands-down the better man. Even in a blind taste test. If he did so say himself.

Sam stepped closer to Mia—clearly intent on a reunion—and Damian sprang into action.

The other guy grasped Mia's hands and lowered his head.

"Mia." Damian made sure his voice cut into the tableau like scissors slicing a photo in half.

Sam froze, and then straightened and turned.

Damian saw it all as if in slow motion. "Thanks for penthouse sitting for me, babe." He winked. "I'll make it up to you this weekend. Reservations at Per Se."

Sam looked between Damian and Mia, and expressions flitted across his face—confusion, dawning understanding and then sheepish embarrassment.

Mia jumped into the void. "Sam, you know—"

"Damian Musil." Damian held out his hand, and after a blink, Sam grasped it.

Damian gave the other guy's hand a firm shake, making eye contact. "Japan. Nice place. I've been to Tokyo myself a couple of times."

Sam's expression wavered between a grimace and a smile. "Yeah, I've been away awhile."

Damian nodded. "Business trips can be a damper that way. You're out of the loop."

"No joke."

Sam turned back toward Mia. "It was nice seeing you, Mia." He shrugged. "The coffee shop was okay, but I'll be sticking to the one on my regular route."

Damian nodded. "Good idea."

"Well, see you around."

After Sam walked off, Damian observed Mia. She watched as Sam mounted a scooter parked farther down the block and took off.

Turning back to him, Mia raised her eyebrows, her gaze clashing with his.

"Territorial?"

Possessive. Maybe a bit jealous. But seriously? Damian raised his eyebrows to mirror hers. "He was your backup plan for the Ruby Ball?"

She lifted her chin. "Nice with the I'm-the-captain-of-industry routine."

"Hey, my quick reflexes let him off easy. Think about how much more embarrassing it would have been if he'd kissed you and then realized the guy who'd just spent the night was right behind him."

"Uh-huh." She looked unconvinced.

There didn't seem to be any end to the obstacle course that led to Mia's door. Her brothers, his family, Carl and now Sam. "Clearly he wasn't watching from the coffee shop window when I kissed you goodbye."

Mia's lips gave a telltale twitch.

"Might have been nice to be able to compare and contrast," she mused.

"Oh, yeah?" he queried, stepping closer. "Maybe my goodbye was too fast."

Damian lowered his gaze to her soft, plump lips. So full of promise. *Just like last night.*

His mouth was a hair's breadth from hers when Mia suddenly sprang back.

"Mom!"

Thirteen

Mia watched with apprehension—horror?—as her mother, who'd emerged from a cab, was handed her bag by the driver.

Damian had turned as well, and she could tell that within seconds he too had processed what was happening at the curb.

She also realized the tableau that she and Damian presented… She'd sprung back from Damian's kiss, but not before her gaze had connected with her mother's over his shoulder.

Now the expressions that flitted across her mother's face had moved from delight and puzzlement to surprise and concern.

"It's only an hour on the shuttle." Her mother's tone was mildly reproachful as she came closer.

"What a…surprise." It was a feeling very similar to what she'd experienced minutes ago at Sam's sudden appearance. Mia resisted the urge to pinch herself and make sure she wasn't dreaming all this.

Her mother smiled brightly. Too brightly. As if Damian wasn't standing right *there*… She set down her overnight bag. "I wanted to come to New York to try some restaurants."

Damian smiled. "Of course. How about Per Se?" He nodded at Mia. "I just mentioned making a reservation."

Her mother blinked. "I've never been, but I want to try it."

Mia looked at Damian as if he was crazy, but he winked at her.

"I know reservations are hard to get, so leave that part to me."

Of course. The perks of having an upwards of nine figure bank account.

She and Damian were taking her mother out to dinner. *No way.*

Damian reached down for her mother's bag. "Since you're planning to stay with Mia, let me take your bag up for you."

Smooth, smooth. Her brother Jordan could take pointers from Damian—even though her sibling had a reputation of gliding instead of walking, on and off the ice.

Mia stopped an eye roll and reluctantly handed her keys to Damian.

As Damian stepped away with the bag, Mia caught the bemused expression on her mother's face.

"I was thinking Eataly for lunch..." Camilla's voice trailed off.

Mia ushered her mother into her work studio and flipped on the lights. The smell of coffee wafted through the air. Mia had loved her mother's gift of an automatic espresso maker on a timer. She'd come to associate the scent with the start of the workday.

Before Mia could do more than prepare two demitasse cups, however, the front door to the studio cracked open and Damian's arm appeared, dangling her keys.

Mia hurried over to collect them and then shut the door.

It was nice of Damian not to intrude this time on what promised to be an awkward family conversation. He was learning...and coming along nicely as, yes, boyfriend material.

She took a deep breath and turned back toward her mother.

Camilla raised her cup of espresso and took a sip. "At least he doesn't have the keys to your apartment."

Mia raised her hands as if to ward off the reproach. "Mom, I didn't lie to you about him. Things have recently...changed."

"Of course." Pause. "And the mothers are always the last to know."

Mia could practically see the thought bubble above her mother's head. *Et tu, Brute?*

In the longstanding sibling game of making sure their parents got only select, carefully filtered information, she'd been behind…until recently. First, Cole and Marisa had sprung a surprise wedding on the family that they'd billed as only an engagement party. Then Rick and Chiara had been expecting a baby…and her mother had gotten the news through the gossip columns. And finally Jordan and Sera had managed to keep their relationship under wraps from the rest of the Serenghettis—at least until Mia had chanced upon them locked in an embrace at cousin Oliver's wedding.

But speaking of relationships… If she was going to legitimize hers with Damian, her mother was the best place to start.

"I'm confused. The last time you said that you and Damian are not a *coppia*."

When her mother set down her espresso cup, Mia took her hands in her own. "You know how you said that Dad wanted to win you over so he arranged another stay for himself at the *albergo*?"

Camilla widened her eyes. "Yes, and I said he stayed at a hotel, not my apartment."

"Just an updated version of the same thing, Mom."

Camilla sighed and searched her face. "And you have your heart set on him, too? Some things with love don't change. Doesn't matter the generation."

"Yes." *I love him.* Mia tested out the words as she dropped her mother's hands. *She'd fallen in love with Damian Musil.* Somehow, she wasn't sure exactly when, he'd snuck into her heart. Once she'd given up the fight against their attraction after the charity dinner two weeks ago—and stopped trying to keep him at a distance—she'd found a kindred soul.

Entrepreneur. Maverick. Risk taker. He'd teased and tantalized until she'd engaged...the enemy. Except she'd discovered she much preferred him as her friend and lover.

Her mother tapped a finger against her lips. "I've waited to be mother of the bride. But this is tricky. *Una situazione delicata*."

"Mom," Mia protested, "Damian hasn't proposed."

Camilla's eyes gleamed. "He will...or you could."

Yes, she could. She'd always prided herself on her forward thinking and independent nature, hadn't she? On always being able to do what her brothers did—though proposing wasn't something that had crossed her mind.

But then she was caught in an uncharacteristic attack of nerves. Because she'd just realized how she felt, but Damian had never indicated—

"I see the way he looks at you, Mia."

Mia cleared her throat. "Yes, well. We'll see how things go, right?" she said brightly. "In the meantime, how are things with you and Dad? How is the budding sommelier?"

Her mother suddenly scowled. "The television personality is fine. He wanted to come to New York with me—"

Ugh. At least it hadn't been *both* her parents

chancing upon her and Damian outside her door in the early morning.

"—but then he understood when I suggested a girls' weekend."

Mia bit the inside of her cheek. Her mother had never been like a girlfriend to her—too strict. Still, ever since Mia had turned twenty-five or so, her mother had fancied herself young at heart. "How about we compromise for now and put you in the role of mother of the fashionista? I'll text Gia. She'd love to see you while you're in town."

Some days were harder than others; they just made you want to run out for a margarita. As she surveyed the scraps of fabric and broken thread littering the floor of her design studio, Mia was thankful that at least it was finally Friday.

Her mother had returned to Welsdale midweek with the unspoken agreement that Camilla would mention nothing about running into Damian—but would nevertheless try to soften her husband and sons' stance toward Mia's involvement with a Musil. It had been only her and her mother for dinner at Per Se since Damian had gotten tied up at the office. The two of them had caught up with Gia for lunch the next day.

But just now, thanks to Katie, Mia was in the midst of sending more samples of her best designs over to *Brilliance*. And everything was in chaos. She had a call shortly with one of her suppliers so that all her raw material would arrive at the manufacturer at the same time. She was also due to speak with a small West Coast boutique chain that stocked her designs. On top of it, she had a meeting with her accountant tomorrow, for which she hadn't yet had time to prepare.

She longed for the days when she could concentrate on sketching and designing—and staring out the window for inspiration. The flow of creative juices had sometimes been slow, but her early career had been very fulfilling. Now, she was juggling more tasks, many of which were business related and not creative.

She mentally shrugged as she zipped a dress into a garment bag. On the plus side, at least she didn't have time to dwell on what was happening up in Welsdale—had her mother had a chance to bring up Damian yet?

Regardless, tonight Mia knew she'd see him. A thrill of anticipation ran up her spine. He was everything she'd been looking for, except she hadn't known it. And she resolved, whatever happened with her family or his, she wouldn't let it interfere with their deepening relationship from here on out.

Sure, it would be great if both the Serenghettis and Musils were on board, but at the end of the day, it was just her and Damian. They had built their own lives in New York, and now they'd become intertwined.

Of course, Damian hadn't said he loved her... A touch of doubt crept into the corners of her mind, and she swept it away. They hadn't talked about commitment even though their relationship was pro-gressing rapidly. Still, it seemed as if they'd known each other forever and a day.

When her cell phone buzzed, and she noticed it was her mother, she nearly groaned aloud. She'd really like to find out if Camilla had broached the subject of Damian now that she was back in Wels-dale, but she had enough to deal with today without adding potentially bad news.

"Hi, Mom. What's up?"

"Mia, my show has been canceled," Camilla said without preamble, sounding distressed.

Mia blinked and stilled. "What? How is that pos-sible?"

"The station has been bought and the new owner wants to take it in a different direction."

"Oh, Mom."

"The new owner is Damian."

"What?" Shock made her voice rise. "Damian?"

"Yes."

"Mom, you must be wrong." *He would have told me. I would have known.*

She hadn't seen him while her mother had been in town, or since then. He'd been traveling and then having late nights at work. But still, a bombshell like this should have merited at least a phone call.

"There is no mistake, Mia," her mother replied, her voice thickening with her Italian accent because she was upset. "Damian owns Alley Kat Media."

"But your station in Welsdale is WBEN-TV."

"It is owned by Alley Kat Media."

Mia groaned. She'd actively avoided asking too many questions about Damian's association with Larry Bensen, because their two families had been rivals for years and she didn't want to seem as if she was on a reconnaissance mission to gather information for the Serenghettis.

Mia closed her eyes on a sigh—hadn't Larry mentioned being in the television business? But she'd never had occasion to mention her last name to Larry—only to Katie—so he'd never had a chance to make the connection between her and her mother.

She felt like an idiot for not putting two and two together.

Mia frowned. It was one thing when Damian's family was going head-to-head in business with hers. It was another for him to cancel her mother's cooking show. *How could he?*

Mia knew that *Flavors of Italy* was her mother's baby. Just like her, Camilla had staked an independent career apart from the family construction business.

Damian should understand better than most people how important realizing a dream like that was—why didn't he? Mia had fought so hard to realize her own dreams—she couldn't bear the idea of Damian stomping on her mother's. And then...had he done it deliberately to get back at the Serenghettis?

Her heart squeezed.

"I have two more episodes to tape," Camilla said, "and then *finito*."

"You're not finished, Mom," Mia reassured her,

though her mind was working feverishly. "This is simply the beginning of a new chapter."

"Mia, I am past sixty."

"Mom, you still have game."

"I have what?"

"This is a temporary setback. I'll speak to Damian. I'm sure this can all be worked out."

There had to be some rational explanation. Because the worst-case scenario was that she'd played into the hands of the Musils in their latest battle against the Serenghettis. She'd helped Damian woo the Bensens—so he could become the new owner of WBEN-TV.

"Your father is very upset. *Wine Breaks with Serg!* is canceled, too—"

"By a Musil." Mia winced inwardly.

So much for thinking her family would come around to liking Damian. She'd been naive to think the two of them could put their family histories behind them.

Fourteen

Mia strode into Damian's glass-enclosed offices on the twenty-third floor of the pre-war building facing Fifth Avenue. New York's Flatiron District had been nicknamed Silicon Alley years ago for all the tech companies with headquarters in the neighborhood, and Damian's company was situated at a marquee address.

After the call from her mother, she'd restrained herself until after the end of the business day. She'd been busy, of course, but she also didn't want a full audience of his employees to witness their confrontation. As it was, it was seven in the evening, and there were still several people milling about the cavernous space. It was a tech company, after all, and long hours were fairly standard. Plus, Mia figured they had plenty of contacts on the West Coast in Silicon Valley, where it was still only four in the afternoon. Still, she couldn't wait forever to get this conversation over with.

The CyberSilver offices were within walking distance of her studio in the Garment District. Since they lived and worked not too far from each other, she hoped the island of Manhattan was big enough for them not to cross paths after this. But given her recent experiences running into Carl and Sam, she had her doubts.

Since Damian's offices were typical for a tech-savvy startup—lots of glass, lots of open space, and lots of windows—it made him easy to spot.

She'd sent a brief text to say that she was on her way.

His response had come while she'd been crossing Sixth Avenue. See you soon, babe.

There hadn't been an inkling that he had a clue that her world had gone topsy-turvy since they'd seen each other at the beginning of the week. She, on the other hand, was bursting with emotion, wanting answers.

When she got to the door of his office, Damian looked up, grinned and rose.

Striding across the carpet, she planted her hands on his desk and leaned forward. "How could you?"

He glanced down at himself. "What? Wrong T-shirt? Fashion faux pas?"

When she continued to fix him with a look, he seemed to realize she wasn't joking.

"You canceled my mother's cooking show."

"What are you talking about?"

She straightened, partly mollified. As unbelievable as it seemed, he looked genuinely perplexed. "My mother has a cooking show on WBEN-TV and its sister stations. And because of her, my father also has a gig fronting related short spots called *Wine Breaks with Serg!* Or should I say *had*. He's been informed that he's kaput, too."

Damian's gaze grew more alert. "You're not kidding."

She pursed her lips. She could see how Damian hadn't necessarily realized the connection to the Serenghettis from the name *Wine Breaks with Serg!* but her mother's show was a different story. "Your lawyers' due diligence didn't reveal that Alley Kat broadcasts *Flavors of Italy with Camilla Serenghetti*?"

"Some junior lawyer must have drilled down to individual shows, but I only get summaries. Of course, I knew there were cooking shows…and I may have seen a list of programming." He frowned. "Probably something called *Flavors of Italy*."

"*Flavors of Italy* is what my mother's show used to be called, and how it's still sometimes referred to. But the name got expanded a few years ago to include identifying the host." Damn it, she was proud of her mother. And it made her so mad that she might have her spatula taken away from her. Especially, Mia admitted, when she herself had inadvertently played a role in bringing the whole thing about.

Damian sighed and came around his desk. "Mia, I had no idea that your mother had a cooking show on WBEN."

She blew a breath—palpable relief coursing through her. "So you won't be canceling her—them?"

He hesitated, his face closing. "That's a business decision. The station is being revamped to focus more on movies and less on original programming."

Hold on. She folded her arms.

"Who produces your mother's show?"

"Signa Entertainment." That much she knew.

"Yeah, that's the company that produces a number of shows on WBEN and Alley Kat's other stations. They're closing shop due to profitability issues."

Mia dropped her arms and raised her chin. "My mother can get another production company. She can even produce it herself. Don't sidestep the issue."

Heck, Mia thought, if she could start her own fashion label, her mother could go the do-it-yourself route, too.

"This isn't personal."

He came around his desk and reached out for her, but she moved away.

The urge to touch him and have him wrap her in his arms—and pretend this whole burgeoning fiasco wasn't happening—was strong. She fought against it.

"Damian," she said in frustration, "it's all personal. Our families have been engaged in a business rivalry for years."

Damian frowned. "So when you came over here, you thought I might be deliberately taking down a Serenghetti?"

Mia shook her head. "It doesn't matter what I thought. Only that you make it right."

He stood there, looking like the gorgeous man she'd snuggled against after a night of spectacular sex, but now acting like a stranger.

Finally, Damian nodded. "Because once a Musil, always a Musil, right?"

How had this conversation gotten off course? Sure she'd had some suspicions, but that was beside the point. Damian could rectify this whole situation with a few strokes of the pen—or taps on the computer keyboard.

"You were prepared to think the worst of me."

Mia shook her head. "Only momentarily—"

"And as long as I make sure the Serenghettis come out okay, all is forgiven? Because your family loyalty overshadows any trust you have in me, right?"

No...wait. What was he saying?

"And what if I decide not to do a favor for the Serenghettis, Mia?" he asked softly. "What would you say?"

She huffed. *Favor?* There was no favor. Her mother had a damn good show. She'd even helped her father find a second act after his stroke—one that Damian had now closed the curtain on.

Damian got a cold, shut-down look on his face. "I think I've got my answer."

And she'd gotten hers. He wasn't going to commit to not canceling. And she wasn't going to grovel. Everything he'd said indicated that he wasn't changing his mind. In fact, he'd made it seem as if *she'd* done something wrong.

Mia blinked. She was flabbergasted. Angry. Annoyed. He was asking her to choose between him and her mother? "I guess there is nothing more to say then, is there?"

They stared at each other a moment longer, and then she swung away and marched out.

Damian raked his hand through his hair and glanced around his empty New York condo.

He'd already been to the gym and for a jog in order to work off excess energy and restlessness. It hadn't helped.

In his penthouse, he was literally and figuratively at the top—at the pinnacle of his life and career— and *alone*. And lonely.

When Mia had left his office last night, he'd been tempted to go after her, but something told him nothing would be accomplished in their current frames of mind. They needed to cool off.

Mia couldn't see this wasn't personal. Yes, it was her mother's cooking show. But since Mia was an entrepreneur herself—one who was used to dealing with financials and the need to turn a profit— she should be able to see it all boiled down to the bottom line.

But he had only himself to blame. He was knee-deep in entanglements with, logically, the last woman he should ever be seriously involved with. If this were purely a business calculation, he should have stopped at *hello* where Mia was concerned.

Tossing aside his usual deliberation, though, he'd pursued his attraction to Mia. Sure, Larry showing up at the Ruby Ball had been an opportunity that had been too good to pass up. But he hadn't stopped to think about his long-term goals with Mia—which was so unlike him.

Still, he wasn't guilty of using her as a pawn to get back at her family, no matter what she thought. But had his attraction to Mia been partly rooted in showing that the Musils were on a par with the Serenghettis? That a Musil was worthy of dating a Serenghetti? Even he couldn't separate out all his motives.

Damn, what a tangle. He paced restlessly. He'd had hours to think and be mad, and it had gotten him nowhere. Now that his annoyance was finally receding, he could think more clearly.

Belatedly, he acknowledged he'd put Mia in an impossible situation of divided loyalty between him and the Serenghettis. No, not just the Serenghettis, but worse—her mother, Camilla Serenghetti, in particular. The one member of Mia's immediate family who seemed to be—maybe—not so dead set against him. Not to mention, he'd handed Mia's father another reason to dislike him. *Way to go, Musil*.

He'd been bothered that Mia had thought he might have masterminded some kind of revenge plan using her as bait. On the other hand, the fact that she'd seemed torn—felt some loyalty to him as well as the rest of the Serenghettis—said something. Their relationship had moved fast…and could get only stronger going forward if they could work through this somehow.

On impulse, Damian picked up his cell phone. He was going to do what he couldn't remember ever doing in his adult life. *Ask his father for advice.*

The irony was, his rapprochement with his father had been facilitated by the Serenghettis—because Mia had helped him court the Bensens. His ownership of WBEN-TV meant he was coming back to Welsdale, which pleased Jakob.

He'd accused Mia of exhibiting loyalty to her family, but he was guilty of the same, he acknowledged ruefully. Still, he needed to get Jakob on board with a plan that was starting to form in his mind.

Damian didn't waste too much time on pleasantries when Jakob picked up. "Dad, I just fired Camilla and Serg Serenghetti from their television jobs."

"What?" The word came out almost as a bark.

Backtracking, he tried to explain the situation as best as he could, finishing with, "What should I do, Dad?"

"Grovel."

"Huh?" It was the last word that he expected to hear from his father's lips.

Jakob grumbled. "Damian, I raised two teenagers as a single parent. Sometimes I worried if I did a good job. So I'll get to the point. Make up with Mia Serenghetti."

Shouldn't his father be...gloating? Expressing some form of satisfaction?

"It's clear that Mia means a lot to you. Your mother died young. Life is short. Hold on to love when you find it."

Huh? Damian cut off a disbelieving laugh. "I expected—"

"I never harbored ill will toward Camilla. In fact, when your mother was alive, they were volunteers together at the soup kitchen."

"Mom never mentioned that."

"You were young, but she did not tell me either. I was shopping with her one day when she said hello to Camilla. She had to tell me how they knew each other."

"I doubt Camilla mentioned it to Serg, either," Damian remarked dryly.

Jakob chuckled. "Serves him right."

That was more like it. "Uh, Dad, you may need to learn to be nice to the Serenghettis."

"I'm counting on being able to learn new tricks." He laughed—a hint of self-satisfaction peeking through.

Damian felt like a huge load had been lifted from his shoulders. "Yeah?"

"I didn't believe that garbage about you and Mia just playing golf together for business."

Damian smiled. "We didn't fool you?"

"Mia likes you or she wouldn't be mad."

Well, *that* made a strange amount of sense.

"One of us has been married. Trust me. And you wouldn't be calling me if you didn't like her."

Damian suddenly heard Valentin in the background and realized he'd caught his father at JM Construction even though it was a Saturday morning. "Why are you at work?"

"Paperwork. Worse every year," Jakob grumbled. "Damn it, Valentin. Did you find that folder?"

In the distance, Damian heard his brother reply, and then his father must have covered the receiver, because there was some indistinct back and forth.

When his father got back on the line, Damian asked, "What did Valentin say?"

"He said you'd better get your rear end back to Welsdale with Mia before the two of us throttle each other at the office. I substituted nicer words for his."

Damian laughed. "I'm looking forward to getting up to Welsdale again soon."

"And I'm going to enjoy Serg learning to be nice to me."

Damian stifled another laugh. He had his marching orders.

Except this was going to be a long, uncertain road. Maybe Mia would be waiting at the end...

If he was lucky.

Fifteen

"He's an underhanded sneak," Mia announced, "and I should have listened to my family."

"Now those are words I never thought would pass your lips," Gia replied.

"What? *Underhanded sneak*?"

"No, *I should have listened to my family.*"

"How could I have been so gullible? So stupid?"

"Stop beating yourself up, Mia. Obviously the two of you have a relationship that's complicated by your last names."

"We have no relationship." She closed her eyes and sucked in a breath. "I haven't spoken to Damian since I confronted him in his office...and he hasn't tried to be in touch."

Two whole days. A whole weekend after the Fri-

ANNA DEPALO

day night massacre at WBEN-TV, when staff had been informed that they were being let go—and told that Damian Musil was the new owner. That much she'd gleaned in follow-up conversations with her mother.

Only dinner with Gia at a local noodle shop was saving her from hiding under her bedcovers—and never, ever coming out. She'd washed the sheets—nothing like a little laundry and mindless housework for the doldrums—but Damian's essence lingered in her apartment. *Damn it.*

Mia swallowed against a stab of pain. Obviously, Damian had had the weekend to think, too, and hadn't reconsidered.

"Oh, come on…"

"No, Gia, really. We had a relationship that was mutually advantageous for business. Now, it isn't anymore."

"Uh-huh."

"Whose side are you on?" she asked sharply. "I thought you said mine."

"You two have a thing for each other. Anyone can see it."

"Thanks. It's nice knowing I'm so transparent. See-through clothing…maybe that's the market niche I've been missing."

Her cousin laughed.

Mia hunched her shoulders and stabbed into her noodle bowl with chopsticks. "Don't humanize him. He's a beast."

"In or out of bed?" Gia's eyes were wide, guileless, but her mouth held a hint of a smirk.

Mia flushed. "I've been the victim of the biggest con of my life."

"He didn't know that he was canceling your parents—"

"But even when he found out, he tried to argue it was all business." Is that what their...relationship had been to him—all business?

Mia's phone buzzed, and she picked it up from the tabletop and scanned the screen. Another text from her brothers—this time Cole. *Ignore*. She hit a button and dropped the cell into the handbag dangling from her chair.

Gia angled her head. "Don't you think your reaction is because you see this as a personal betrayal?"

"What?" she scoffed.

"If Damian cared for you, he'd abandon his plans for the television station."

"You don't pull any punches, Gia," she joked.

Mia's heart squeezed. Her cousin was right. She was in love with Damian. It had happened without her knowing. He'd sneaked in. And now she'd gotten evidence that he didn't give a damn.

On the other hand, a little voice in her head whispered, if she cared about him—*loved him*—wouldn't she support him in doing what was best for his business? Even at the expense of her family?

What a mess. She couldn't really accuse Damian of not valuing their relationship without looking a wee bit hypocritical. Except she did think her mother had a damn good show—if only Damian could see that himself.

The dizzying mix of emotions slammed into her, and she grasped for something solid to steady her.

"I need to help my mother," she said resolutely.

With sudden clarity, Mia realized her family needed her at this moment as much as they thought she needed them. If anything, she could make a last-ditch effort to save her mother's show by demonstrating it was worth saving.

"Well, I don't see what you can do about it, short of blackmailing Damian."

"I'm the only one of my siblings who hasn't made a recent appearance on my mother's show, and now it's over. What's the saying? Make time for the important things in life?"

"Doesn't she have any shows left to tape?"

"One or two."

"Then get yourself up to Welsdale and put your misplaced guilt to rest."

Mia worried her bottom lip, because Gia had given voice to an idea that had started germinating in her own head. "You're right. It might not change things but—"

"You have a beautiful memory to make with your mother."

Yup. On the other hand, all of her memories with Damian were likely in the past…even if her appearance on her mother's show convinced him to keep it on the air.

* * *

Fortunately, it hadn't been hard to run Rick Serenghetti to ground. With a few phone calls back and forth between assistants, Damian had been able to determine that Mia's brother was in New York for business.

He'd been prepared to fly out to Los Angeles if necessary. Luck, it seemed, was on his side—at least this time. It had gone AWOL for a while.

Now he was finally meeting the middle Serenghetti brother in the lounge of a swanky Midtown hotel.

Rick eyed him from across a small table. This corner of the ground floor lounge was empty at four in the afternoon.

"You know," Rick mused, "I debated whether to meet you."

"I appreciate your time."

Rick shrugged, his casualness belied by the indecipherable look on his face. "But then I figured I had the chance to get a jump start on my brothers in laying into you."

Damian grimaced. He couldn't blame the guy when he'd managed to lay off his parents and break up with his sister in the same week. If it had been Cole, a physical altercation might have been a more serious possibility, but Rick remained cool as a cucumber. Damian chalked it up to nerves of steel honed as a movie stunt man. "Hear me out."

"Chiara convinced me that I should. She seems to think you may have some redeeming qualities."

"Good to know the Serenghetti in-laws aren't quite as—"

"—hostile as Mia's brothers?" Rick lounged back and rested his arm along the back of the cushioned bench seat. "I heard Mia prevented you from being hustled out the door in Welsdale by Cole and Jordan. Crashing family get-togethers is your thing?"

Damian rubbed his jaw—which had emerged from that meeting still in good shape. "Yeah, but the Musils and Serenghettis are no longer competing to acquire the same construction company since Tevil Construction took itself off the market. So two steps forward for Serenghetti-Musil relations right there."

"Two little steps…and one big one back, too, since then."

"I'm rectifying it."

Rick raised his eyebrows, looking intrigued.

In preparation for today's meeting, Damian had watched a marathon of old *Flavors of Italy* episodes. It seemed a lot had been going on in Welsdale since he'd moved away, and the show definitely had its appealing qualities. It was also clearly a family affair, with Camilla bringing on assorted relatives and even their spouses as guests—until Damian had brought down the butcher knife and cut off any more episodes.

Still, watching the show had proved to be a good way to get to know the Serenghettis. He'd been entertained by Cole obviously salivating over his future wife, Marisa. Jordan had vied against his own hockey teammates on a cook-off that Sera had judged. And even Rick had been teased on screen when his then-girlfriend, Chiara, had been a guest. Of course, Damian had eaten up every crumb of Mia's appearance on a couple of the early episodes, when she'd looked as edible as the Italian cream pastry that she was helping to prepare...

Before Damian could lay out his plan for Rick, however, an attractive woman walked in holding the hand of a boy who looked to be close to Dahlia's age.

Even dressed casually in a striped sundress, with a pair of shades obscuring her eyes, Damian recognized the actress Chiara Feran. He'd seen the news when her romance with Rick Serenghetti had become public a few years ago.

As Rick stood, Damian followed suit.

"Vincent wanted to go for a walk," Chiara announced with a smile, "so we're heading to the park for a bit."

Rick's face softened, and he hunched down. "Hey, bud, take it easy with the stunts on the playground equipment, okay?"

Vincent looked gleeful. "Stunts, stunts."

Chiara sighed. "Like father, like son."

Damian glanced at her. "Looks like the next generation of Serenghettis is all cute."

"You've met Dahlia then, I take it?" she answered with a smile.

"Let's just say she was the most welcoming of the Serenghettis on that occasion."

As Chiara laughed, he held out his hand. "I'm Damian Musil."

"Chiara Feran," she supplied, shaking his hand. "I've heard so much about you."

Rick hooked the tops of his hands into his pockets. "Is this really about taking Vincent for a walk?"

Chiara shot her husband an amused look. "Just taking a small detour to say goodbye to you before we're on our way."

"Musil is still in one piece, as you can see," Rick muttered.

Chiara's lips twitched.

Damian figured that Chiara had done more than a little convincing to persuade her husband that this meeting was worthwhile. For some reason, Mia's sisters-in-law were ready to throw him a lifeline. But then he assumed it took women as strong as Mia to handle the Serenghetti brothers.

Rick ruffled his son's hair.

"Well, we'll be going then," Chiara said lightly.

Rick brushed her lips in a light kiss. "You look great, and I'm glad you're dressed for the weather. It's hot out there."

"Happy you like the dress." Chiara threw a significant glance at Damian. "It's a Mia Serenghetti design. Isn't it fantastic?"

Smoothly done.

Chiara turned, leading Vincent away. "Enjoy... your talk."

Rick said something under his breath as both he and Damian took their seats again.

"Looks like the Serenghettis may have another stunt man in their midst."

"Not if Chiara can help it," Rick supplied shortly. "But since we're on the topic, what's the purpose of this stunt you're pulling? I mean, this meeting."

"I've got a proposition, and I need your help."

"And I've got a news flash for you," Rick responded dryly. "Serenghettis and Musils don't help each other."

"They don't date each other, either."

Rick's gaze flickered for an instant. "A lapse in judgment on my sister's part that I hear she's since rectified."

"Then why did you agree to meet me? Aside from Chiara's influence, that is."

Rick's gaze flickered again. "I'm not supposed to say this, but Mia is torn up. She blames herself for my parents'...predicament."

Damian felt like a jerk. "I want to make things right with Mia."

"I don't think that's possible."

Yeah. But Damian had dealt with long odds before.

"Once my sister has made up her mind, it's hard, if not impossible, to change it."

"I know."

"So you must be delusional or—"

"I care about her." *I can't stop thinking about her. I want to be with her.*

Rick regarded him silently but eventually sighed. "Okay, spill it."

"I want you to help your mother start her own production company."

Rick said nothing for a few seconds. "Nice, but where will the show be slotted?" he probed. "An online streaming service?"

"I want to keep broadcasting *Flavors of Italy* but I'd like the show to get a fresher look. The goal is to grow the audience but keep the name of the program." He'd gleaned a few things from watching Camilla's show, not only as a viewer, but also as a shrewd entrepreneur.

Rick played with an empty coaster on the table. "You know, I was mulling the idea of having the Serenghettis produce the show ourselves. I own a production company, but it's only dealt with feature films up to now. It'd be better if my mother was set up with her own shop."

Great. If Camilla had a new production company, the problem would be solved—or half solved. Damian could deal with the rest from his end.

"But why would we need you?" Rick asked pointedly. "My mother could get broadcast anywhere."

"I'm assuming your mother still attaches some value to being on her hometown station. On the channel where she started and viewers are used to seeing her."

"Right, the Welsdale station that you now own. A fact you didn't share with my sister."

"I didn't know about the Serenghetti connection." *Had Mia mentioned that part?* Then he shrugged. "I'm not much of a cooking show kind of guy."

"If you hang around my sister much longer, you will be."

That's what I'm counting on.

"Well, we agree on one thing," Rick conceded. "My mother needs her own production company."

Mia's brother hadn't exactly agreed to cooperate, but he'd given Damian an opening.

One Damian was ready to make the most of. He needed Rick to persuade the other Serenghettis... *Time to seal the deal.*

Sixteen

For her last show, Camilla announced that she wanted to make a millefoglie Italian wedding cake.

Mia mentally shrugged. She thought the choice was a little odd, but maybe her mother was putting the best face on a bad situation with her trademark optimistic style.

"We will assemble the cake right here," her mother said, speaking to the camera, "and with the help of some special guests."

Guests? As far as Mia was aware, she was the only guest.

"*Mia figlia*, Mia Serenghetti...and the new owner of this television station, Damian Musil."

The audience clapped.

Stunned, Mia watched Damian stride onto the set.

What was he doing here? Still, her bewildered senses feasted on him. He was tall, commanding... and seemingly relaxed. He looked as good, if not better, than when she'd last seen him. Dark hair, bedroom eyes, chiseled features, and muscled body in slacks and an open-collar shirt. Her heart felt a pang. He'd have a new girlfriend in no time.

When they'd last parted, he'd been cool and distant. Now he was all smiles and insouciance.

Fortunately, the TV camera wasn't trained on her at the moment, so she had an instant to compose herself.

She soon narrowed her eyes fractionally at her mother. What was she up to? Or had Damian demanded to be put on air—so it wouldn't seem like he was the bad guy who'd ended the show? Someone had some explaining to do...

Mia cut off the flow of thoughts racing through her head. Because there was no more time to think. Because Damian was up on stage, standing beside her, joining her and her mother in the worst cooking show casting *ever*.

While the camera focused on Camilla, Mia leaned slightly toward Damian. "What are you doing here?"

"Lending a hand," he muttered back, keeping his smile in place.

"And your good name."

"Something for everyone," he replied easily. "Smile for the camera, Mia."

"For a Musil, you sure go out of your way to associate with Serenghettis," Mia responded in a low voice, while her mother continued her explanation of baking for the benefit of the studio audience and the television cameras.

Damian glanced at her, his eyes gleaming. "Maybe you've changed my mind."

Mia felt heat stamp her face. *At least they weren't live.* If necessary, she could muscle her way into the production room later, and beg and plead for some strategic editing.

But first, she had to survive this taping. She'd already downgraded her expectations from helping to make this episode her mother's best ever to…surviving. *Wonderful.*

After a producer trotted on stage to outfit Damian with a microphone, she and Damian worked together under her mother's direction to mix the ingredients. *Why, oh why, did it have to be a wedding cake?*

It was a running family joke that her brothers and their wives had appeared on Camilla's show and soon after had gotten married. *Well, she and Damian were about to break the mold.*

Mia wasn't sure how she was going to make it through today. It was like the heat of a thousand suns. The audience…her family…the wedding theme… *Damian.* If she was still standing at the end of this episode, she'd plunge headfirst into the cake…

"Now Damian, Mia has helped me in the kitchen before, so you are the *secondo assistente, sì*?"

Mia nearly rolled her eyes.

"*Millefoglie* means a thousand layers in *italiano*,"

202 SO RIGHT...WITH MR. WRONG

Camilla said. "The millefoglie wedding cake is *molto popolare in Italia*."

Mia scanned the audience, and her gaze came to rest on her family, including her father and brothers, sitting in the back. Why was no one glowering at Damian? Or better yet, jumping on stage to start an argument, so the show could go off the air with a real bang? Maybe they were all here to support her mother no matter what?

"First we will mix the ingredients for the vanilla custard," Camilla continued. "Then we will assemble with layers of pastry and fresh berries."

"Sounds delicious," Damian chimed in.

"Now a little birdie told me that you like strawberries, Damian, so we will make this cake with those in addition to blueberries and raspberries."

"Thank you."

"Prego."

Mia nearly gagged.

"I am showing everyone how to make the cake today, but," Camilla added, "I've never had a personal opportunity. You know, I've never been the mother of the bride."

Mia wondered with chagrin what the heck she'd been thinking by agreeing to appear on her mother's last episode...

"Have you ever had millefoglie, Damian?" Camilla asked benignly.

"No, I haven't. I've never been married," he joked.

Camilla tittered and then winked. "Maybe Mia can help you at the end."

They both turned to look at Mia.

The audience murmured, and Mia pasted a tight smile on her face. What had she been saying about ending with a bang? Apparently, though, her mother had the drama angle covered all by herself.

"Sure," she said brightly. "Why not let Damian have his cake and eat it, too?"

The audience gasped and chuckled while Damian had the audacity to laugh at her with his eyes.

Seriously, what was her mother thinking?

When they were finished making the cake, Mia almost sagged with relief.

"Mia, why don't you offer Damian a taste?" Camilla asked, looking into the camera.

In slow motion, Mia cut into an edge of the cake with a large spoon. Then bracing herself, she offered Damian a sample.

Damian obligingly opened his mouth—but the look in his eyes said he'd rather eat her up. *Gia had called that one.*

When Damian swallowed his bite, Camilla asked, "How do you like it?"

"It's delicious," he said with a smile, his gaze on Mia. "With any luck, I'll have one at my own wedding someday."

Mia kept a smile stuck on her face, but she wondered whether the cameras could pick up on the fact that she was being consumed by heat. Just a couple more minutes, and her mother would give her signature signoff...

"And now, I have big news," Camilla said.

Mia's gaze swiveled to her mother. *Please, no.* She didn't think she could take any more surprises.

Surely her mother wasn't going to announce the cancellation of her show right now? Right next to Damian? Right when Mia was imagining herself melting under the hot lights like so much gelatinous custard sitting in the sun too long?

"I have started my own production company," Camilla said with a flourish. "Dolci Productions. Now *Flavors of Italy* will have a new look." Her mother scanned the audience. "Thanks *mille* to my son, Rick Serenghetti, who helped arrange this."

A television camera panned to Rick in the audience. Her brother gave a slight smile and nod, while Serg, Colé and Jordan all looked over at him in acknowledgment.

So her mother hoped to keep the show going somehow with her own company? Was that why her family was content to sit in the audience? Mia's spirits lifted, and she stopped herself from throwing an unbeaten look in Damian's direction.

Her mother glanced beyond her to Damian, as if to give him his cue, but her expression was happy instead of victorious.

"Even though this is the last episode of the current program, Camilla will be back on-air next season with a whole new look for *Flavors of Italy*."

Mia blinked at Damian. She'd heard what he'd said, but it wasn't processing. Still, she was able to note her father looking pleased in the audience.

"*Alla prossima volta*," Camilla ended gaily. "Till next time, *buon appetito*."

Wait...*what?* On air...where?

As soon as the cameras went off, Mia worked on detaching her mic.

"Fantastic chemistry during this episode," one of the producers announced loudly, striding toward them. "We should have these two guests on together again soon."

Never. She didn't think she could survive it.

As her mother and Damian were waylaid by the producer, Mia hurried from the stage. She had a million questions, but right now she had to get away from Damian.

She didn't know whether to laugh or cry. Sure, her mother's show had been saved, but she and Damian were still canceled...

Hurrying along a backstage hallway, Mia heard footsteps behind her and then glanced over her shoulder.

"Mia, stop," Damian insisted.

"Forget it."

"I need to talk to you," he said, catching up with her.

She stopped. "No."

He opened the nearest door as if he hadn't heard her. "In here will do."

"Your new office? How does it feel to be the owner of the station?" She had to protect her vulnerable heart.

"Fantastic. I thought I'd add a fashion show to the weekly lineup. You know, up-and-comers competing against each other."

"I'm sure you'll be able to find plenty of gullible designers with a penchant for Robin Hood costumes."

He had the audacity to chuckle. "You think so? Maybe I'll need some help."

She was done with offering him assistance...

They were attracting looks from staffers passing them in the hallway, so Mia chose the lesser evil and marched past him into the room. "Wouldn't a show along the lines of *Shark Bait* be more your speed? Every week people can tune in to see which competitor survives with their dreams intact."

He smiled and closed the door.

She stabbed a finger in his direction. "Did you enjoy your star turn on my mother's show?"

He opened his mouth, but she wasn't finished. "I sure hope so. Because she's poured her heart and soul into it."

"The cake was delicious—"

"I'm glad you agree." She placed her hands on her hips and cocked her head. "I was imagining you wearing it."

"I'm not sure berry is my color."

"Oh, it is. Take it from me." She pinned him with a look. "I've studied fashion, and what's trending right now is shades of red." *She was on fire.*

Damian quirked his lips. "I thought my acting

skills were fairly good, even if it was just a cooking show."

"*Just* a cooking show?" She took a deep breath to brace herself. "This may not mean much to you, but my mother spent years being the behind-the-scenes supporter of a husband and four kids. Finally, she had time to pursue her dream, her second act, and what do you do? You—"

"Keep her on WBEN-TV as well as its sister stations, and invest in her new production company?"

She stared at him blankly for a moment and then blinked.

"She's staying in her time slot with a revamped look for the show. Same name though."

"What?" She dropped her hands from her hips. So her mother wasn't only staying on-air with her own production company, she was going to continue to be broadcast on her regular station—where she already had an audience.

"I offered her a deal before today's show." He smiled. "Before I had my acting skills tested. Fortunately, I could mostly be myself since it was a reality-based show."

"You've been in negotiations with—" what had her mother called it? "—Dolci Productions."

"Not only that. I contacted Rick to talk about setting up the new company. With any luck, both of us can work out an even better syndication deal for her. She'll reach a wider market."

"How did I not know this?"

"I wanted to work behind the scenes." His lips

quirked up again. "I've found that's best where the Serenghettis are concerned."

She waved her arms inanely. "My whole family was in the audience."

"I asked them not to say anything. Though your father was bursting to mention something about *Wine Breaks with Serg!* becoming its own spin-off show."

Good—her father needed his own turf, for both his and her mother's sakes. "So you swore them to silence...for the grand gesture?"

He nodded, rubbing the back of his neck. "I thought they'd enjoy watching a Musil brought to his knees."

She swallowed, her throat suddenly dry. "Why?"

He sauntered closer. "Don't you know?"

"Know what?"

He lowered his eyes, concealing his gaze. "I did it for you."

Mia studied his mouth. He was so close, her world had narrowed to him and what he was saying.

"For us."

She shook her head mutely—vestiges of a fight still in her. "There is no us."

"There could be."

She gave a nervous laugh. "Until the next time you cancel my mother's show?"

There were so many obstacles...and if she tried very hard right now, she'd remember some of them.

"I want you."

"And what Damian Musil wants, Damian Musil

gets, is that it?" she huffed—because she was afraid to hope.

."No. I can't make you want me."

Oh… Her gaze traveled up to lock with his. "Stop poking holes in my reasons—"

"Love me, Mia."

"You—"

He wrapped his arms around her and covered her mouth with his.

The kiss was needy, desperate… She sighed against his lips, opening herself, and then shifted restlessly against him in order to get closer.

When he started to get aroused, they finally and reluctantly broke apart.

"I love you."

He softly brushed his lips against hers. "You're my heart."

She sighed against his mouth. "When I heard that my mother's show was being canceled, I assumed you were waging war on the Serenghettis."

"Shh, it's okay," he soothed, rubbing her arms. "You were upset."

She searched his gaze. "I couldn't believe I didn't figure out the business between you and Larry involved WBEN-TV. I was embarrassed…humiliated…and hurt for my parents—my mother in particular. They'd warned me about you, and I didn't listen. It seemed as if they'd been right all along, and I'd lived up to the image of rebellious Mia who doesn't know better."

He caressed the pulse at the side of her neck, the

motion soothing. "Corporate holdings can be complicated and convoluted, and you were distracted by the potential fashion angle with Katie. Besides, I didn't put two and two together, either, and make the connection between your family and WBEN."

She smiled. "Because you're not into cooking shows."

The side of his mouth lifted.

Mia's smile turned tentative. "There will be other times when our families may clash. After all, the Musils and Serenghettis continue to be business rivals."

"And now that I'm your mother's boss, it's even more complicated, but it will never be boring," he teased.

"You can joke about it?"

He rested his forehead against hers. "I've moved boulders already for us to be together, Mia."

She widened her eyes and pulled back to search his.

He shrugged, the nonchalant movement belying the intensity of his expression. "I've been attracted to you for a long time, and it was clear you weren't going to give me an opening. A guy can only be so patient."

She swatted him playfully. "What attraction?"

He raised a brow. "I even envied Carl when he was dating you. When he started exploring other jobs, it was a relief."

"And you helped him walk out the door."

He nodded. "Guilty. Let's just say I had no problem providing a letter of recommendation."

"The way you helped him find another girlfriend, too?" she asked archly.

Damian looked uncharacteristically and endearingly abashed. "I know that your feelings were hurt. I'd never have helped if—"

She touched a finger to his lips. "You were right. Carl and I would never have lasted. But I was too busy being mad at you for your role at the time to want to acknowledge it."

He kissed her finger before she moved it away. "Why are we talking about Carl?"

"Because you had the hots for me."

"And you didn't feel any spark of attraction ever?" he joked.

She caressed his jaw, unable to keep herself from touching him. "With our families, it always seemed like a bad idea to do any exploration where you were concerned."

He gave her a peck on the lips. "We'll work it out. Your family were all in on the plan for today's cooking show, so things are looking good already."

"All of them?" she gasped.

"Well, your mother and Rick put the word out."

"I can't believe they all showed up today."

"They want to see you happy. I think that convinced them."

"You convinced them that you'd make me happy," she teased.

"Okay, guilty." His eyes crinkled. "I think they

were impressed that I braved the Serenghetti lair for you the last time we were in Welsdale."

"Why didn't you tell me before the taping?"

"Plan A was to show up before the show to talk to you," he admitted. "But I got stalled in New York on business."

"Oh!" No wonder everyone had been able to keep Damian's appearance a secret. He'd only just arrived.

"The season finale was supposed to end with my declaration of undying love for you. But without hashing things out with you first, I wasn't sure how you'd react."

The hint of vulnerability was her undoing.

"Your brothers missed out on witnessing that part."

Her heart squeezed. "Well, for my part, I'm not sure I'm up to the job of taking on the Musils." At Damian's surprised look, she added lightly, "I've had a hard enough time dealing with my brothers, and the Musils have their share of testosterone floating around."

Damian gave a lopsided smile, and then he wrapped her arms around his waist. "You're up to the challenge, don't worry. You'll have them tamed in no time."

"Aren't you supposed to be the tamer, with your name?" she teased.

"You can teach me all you know."

"Starting right now."

And then when Damian flipped the lock on the door, Mia gave herself up to being the biggest Serenghetti rebel of all...by loving a Musil.

Epilogue

The big Serenghetti family wedding was finally happening. Cole and Marisa had surprised everyone by turning their engagement party into a wedding. Rick and Chiara had had quick nuptials because Chiara was pregnant. And even Jordan and Sera had done a hasty scaled-down affair to coincide with the hockey off-season and in order to avoid too much press coverage.

Mia surveyed the proceedings. It was a fashion and culinary showcase all in one. Her desires and her mother's tastes had dovetailed nicely. At last, Camilla had found an offspring who was into the same fantasy wedding that she was.

Thanks to Katie's connections, Mia's wedding was also the cover story for an upcoming issue of

Wedding Bells magazine. And of course, there was a millefoglie wedding cake complete with strawberries as well as raspberries and blueberries—because everyone knew the groom liked it that way.

Mia's gown was an ivory Chantilly lace with an off-the-shoulder bodice. She'd surprised even herself by going traditional. But then she'd added spectacular aquamarine teardrop earrings that Damian had gifted her for something blue, as well as the headpiece that her mother had worn at her own wedding to hold her veil. She'd borrowed her sister-in-law Chiara's diamond hair clips to hold her hair back. She'd even done the traditional Italian candied almond wedding favors, thanks to her mother's input.

Her engagement ring was an understated diamond that had been among the items in the box that Jakob Musil had given his son months ago in JM Construction's office. It turned out that Damian's mother had passed along her engagement ring to her son in addition to letters and other mementos. Mia treasured it as a gift from the mother-in-law she'd never get to know but who lived on through Damian.

The ring had even surpassed Damian's other surprise—because his wedding gift to her had turned out to be all the jewelry that she'd gotten on loan, including the ruby pieces that she'd loved and worn for the Ruby Ball, and the diamonds that she'd put on for the charity dinner. He'd never gotten around to returning them, and had claimed with a wink that he'd decided to make an investment in jewelry instead.

As the band struck up, Damian claimed her hand.

The lights in the reception hall dimmed, and she and Damian walked onto the dance floor and swayed to "Wonderful Tonight."

"Special request to the band," Damian murmured.

She felt chills race down her spine—as she often did around him.

Damian looked over her shoulder and scanned the ballroom around them. "Looks as if everyone is behaving."

"The photographer and writer from *Wedding Bells* are here. Plus, my mother read my brothers the riot act. She's finally got her turn as the mother of the bride, and she's going to show highlights on *Flavors of Italy*."

"Naturally," Damian deadpanned.

Mia smiled fondly at the two babies asleep in strollers in a quiet corner of the ballroom. Even her new nephews were apparently cooperating in making sure that the wedding went off without a hitch. Sergio had Cole's dark hair and hazel eyes, while Marco was fairer, as if Sera's blond locks and Jordan's darker hue had been mixed together. And now Rick and Chiara were expecting again, too—this time a girl.

Mia spied her father sitting at a table and chatting with Jakob Musil. "It seems my mother didn't have to worry about our fathers, either. They're chummy these days."

Damian followed her gaze and then smiled. "All is forgiven when your construction companies have joined forces and your kids are getting married to each other."

Serenghetti Construction had partnered with JM Construction to bid for more and bigger projects than either could handle alone. Though neither had ended up buying Tevil Construction, they'd found a way to work together to achieve the same benefits the purchase would have imparted.

"Next thing we know, they'll be playing bocce ball together," Mia remarked lightly.

"I've got news for you. They already have."

Mia threw back her head and laughed.

"You're wonderful tonight and every night," Damian murmured as the singer crooned the song's romantic refrain and other couples joined them.

"Remember how you felt that way when we have our next argument," she teased.

He quirked an eyebrow. "I thought we put all that behind us."

"We haven't gone through your closet yet."

He laughed. "I forgot. I'm now a fashion designer's accessory."

"My best accessory," she said firmly. "And my husband, lover—"

He swept his lips across hers. "Don't forget life partner."

Yes. Yes to everything. Yes to finally finding each other.

* * * * *

*Don't miss a single story
in The Serenghetti Bothers series!*

**Second Chance with the CEO
Hollywood Baby Affair
Power Play
So Right…with Mr. Wrong**

from USA TODAY *bestselling author
Anna DePalo!*

Available now from Harlequin Desire!

WE HOPE YOU ENJOYED
THIS BOOK FROM
 HARLEQUIN
DESIRE

*Luxury, scandal, desire—welcome to
the lives of the American elite.*

Be transported to the worlds of oil barons, family dynasties,
moguls and celebrities. Get ready for juicy plot twists,
delicious sensuality and intriguing scandal.

6 NEW BOOKS AVAILABLE EVERY MONTH!

#2803 THE TROUBLE WITH BAD BOYS
Texas Cattleman's Club: Heir Apparent
by Katherine Garbera

Landing bad boy influencer Zach Benning to promote Royal's biggest soiree is a highlight for hardworking Lila Jones. And the event's marketing isn't all that's made over! Lila's sexy new look sets their relationship on fire... Will it burn hot enough to last?

#2804 SECOND CHANCE COUNTRY
Dynasties: Beaumont Bay • by Jessica Lemmon

Country music star Cash Sutherland hasn't seen Presley Cole since he broke her heart. Now a journalist, she's back in his life and determined to get answers he doesn't want to give. Will their renewed passion distract her from the truth?

#2805 SEDUCTION, SOUTHERN STYLE
Sweet Tea and Scandal • by Cat Schield

When Sienna Burns gets close to CEO Ethan Watts to help her adopted sister, she's disarmed by his Southern charm, sex appeal...and insistence on questioning her intentions. Now their explosive chemistry has created divided loyalties that may derail all her plans...

#2806 THE LAST LITTLE SECRET
Sin City Secrets • by Zuri Day

It's strictly business when real estate developer Nick Breedlove hires interior designer—and former lover—Samantha Price for his new project. Sparks fly again, but Samantha is hiding a secret. And when he learns the truth about her son, she may lose him forever...

#2807 THE REBEL HEIR
by Niobia Bryant

Handsome restaurant heir Coleman Cress has always been rebellious—in business and in relationships. Sharing a secret no-strings affair with confident Cress family chef Jillian Rossi is no different. But when lust becomes something more, can their relationship survive meddling exes and family drama?

#2808 HOLLYWOOD EX FACTOR
LA Women • by Sheri WhiteFeather

Security specialist Zeke Mitchell was never interested in the spotlight. When his wife, Margot Jensen, returns to acting, their marriage ends...but the attraction doesn't. As things heat up, are the problems of their past too big to overlook?

"Did you expect me to sleep in here with you?"

And there it was. The line that he hadn't thought to draw
but now was obvious he'd need to draw.

He eased back on the bed, shoved a pillow behind his
back and curled her into his side. Arranging the blankets
over both of them, he leaned over and kissed her wild hair,
smiling against it when he thought about the tangles she'd
have to comb out later. He hoped she thought of why they
were there when she did.

"We should talk about that, yeah?" he asked rhetorically.
He felt her stiffen in his arms. "I want you here, Pres. In this
bed. Naked in my arms. I want you on my dock, driving me
wild in that tiny pink bikini. But we should be clear about
what this is…and what it's not."

She shifted and looked up at him, her blue eyes wide and
innocent, her lips pursed gently. "What it's not."

"Yeah, honey," he continued, gentler than before. "What
it's not."

"You mean…" She licked those pink lips and rested a hand tenderly on his chest. "You mean you aren't going to marry me and make an honest woman out of me after that?"

Cash's face broadcasted myriad emotions. From what Presley could see, they ranged from regret to nervousness to confusion and finally to what she could only describe as "oh, shit." That was when she decided to let him off the hook.

Chuckling, she shoved away from him, still holding the sheet to her chest. "God, your face! I'm kidding. Cash, honestly."

He blinked, held that confused expression a few moments longer and then gave her a very unsure half smile. "I knew that."

"I'm not the girl you left at Florida State," she told him. "I grew up, too, you know. I learned how the world worked. I experienced life beyond the bubble I lived in."

She took his hand and laced their fingers together. She still cared about him, so much. After that, she cared more than before. But she also wasn't so foolish to believe that sex—even earth-shattering sex—had the power to change the past. The past was him promising to wait for her and then leaving and never looking back.

"That was really fun," she continued. "I had a great time. You looked like you had a great time. I'm looking forward to doing it again if you're up to the task."

Don't miss what happens next in…
Second Chance Love Song
by Jessica Lemmon, the second book in the
Dynasties: Beaumont Bay series!

Available May 2021 wherever
Harlequin Desire books and ebooks are sold.

Harlequin.com